Suicide Watch

Kelley York

SUICIDE WATCH

Copyright © 2012 Kelley York
All rights reserved.

ISBN-13: 978-1481239035
ISBN-10: 1481239031

Go Away. I'm all right.
– H. G. Wells

SUICIDE WATCH

Table of Contents

JUNE
Chapter 1	Pg 09
Chapter 2	Pg 17
Chapter 3	Pg 25
Chapter 4	Pg 33
Chapter 5	Pg 39

JULY
Chapter 6	Pg 47
Chapter 7	Pg 49

AUGUST
Chapter 8	Pg 61

SEPTEMBER
Chapter 9	Pg 69
Chapter 10	Pg 73
Chapter 11	Pg 75
Chapter 12	Pg 85
Chapter 13	Pg 89
Chapter 14	Pg 93
Chapter 15	Pg 101
Chapter 16	Pg 111

OCTOBER
Chapter 17	Pg 117
Chapter 18	Pg 123
Chapter 19	Pg 125
Chapter 20	Pg 131
Chapter 21	Pg 135
Chapter 22	Pg 141
Chapter 23	Pg 145
Chapter 24	Pg 149

NOVEMBER
Chapter 25	Pg 163
Chapter 26	Pg 167
Chapter 27	Pg 175
Chapter 28	Pg 177
Chapter 29	Pg 179
Chapter 30	Pg 195

DECEMBER
Chapter 31	Pg 209
Acknowledgments	Pg 217
About the Author	Pg 219

SUICIDE WATCH

//Kelley York

June

SUICIDE WATCH

CHAPTER 1

Last Christmas Eve, I watched a girl throw herself off the Woodshire Bridge.

I didn't know her. I'd never seen her around town or anything.

(Though it's not like I get out much.)

She was a stranger I happened to see during my early morning jog, a mile and a half from home.

Not raining, but cold and wet. I stopped at the end of the bridge beneath the shadows of dew-dripping trees, and watched. She didn't notice me. Or maybe she noticed and simply didn't care. By that point, I'm not sure she cared about much of anything. She had on a plaid jacket and black pants, her blonde hair tangled, whipping around her face as she slung her legs over the guard rail. The ledge on the other side wasn't even wide enough for her feet, so she clung to the railing behind her and stared down into the abyss.

At first glance, I had no idea what she was doing. The idea seemed too bizarre, too out there. But I'd heard of people jumping off the bridge. It was prime suicide territory. A newer, wider, sturdier bridge was built closer to the main roads, leaving the Woodshire Bridge pretty abandoned. I've heard how the drop is so high that a body shatters on impact with the water. Even if that didn't kill you, you wouldn't be in any shape to swim and the river would swallow you up. The idea terrified me, but the jumping girl wasn't afraid. From where I stood, I could see her face, and she was so...

Peaceful.

As her hands started to uncurl from the rail, I stepped forward to call after her, to say...I don't know.

Something. Anything.

SUICIDE WATCH

"*Hey!*"

My voice wavered, but there was no way she couldn't have heard me.

She stopped, one hand still on the rail, the other hanging free, and looked at me. She didn't say a word, but waited to see what I wanted as though I'd flagged her down on the street to ask for directions.

In that moment, I should've said a lot of things. I should've asked her why she wanted to die, if living really was *that bad*. If I could do anything to change her mind and did she realize the number of bones she would break by jumping and...

None of those things came to mind.

I asked, "What's your name?"

My question startled her. Of all the things, right? And at first I thought she wouldn't respond until she finally said, "Jessica."

Jessica. Jessica the Jumper. I swallowed hard.

"Don't you think someone will miss you, Jessica?"

Her smile was a distant. Muscle memory. Not truly reaching her eyes. "No one will miss me. You'll see."

She spread her arms wide and jumped.

I never saw her hit the water; she vanished into the fog.

Jessica was right. I searched the papers both online and offline for any mention of a girl who leapt off the bridge. No missing person's report, no obituary, no found body, nada. The world kept turning. Jessica the Jumper was gone and nobody cared. And yet, she'd looked so relaxed and at peace. She was grateful to be getting the hell out of this world and into whatever lies beyond. Her sadness is over.

Since then, I've thought a lot about her. Anytime I get stressed out, I remember her face and I breathe deep, in and out, in and out, trying to find within myself that calm state of being she'd achieved just before death. Sometimes it works. Sometimes, it doesn't.

At this particular moment in time, it fails miserably.

Even when I'm standing in front of an auditorium full of people alongside my graduating class — which consists of a whopping thirty people — I'm thinking about Jessica. I wonder how old she was. If she graduated, or had plans of graduating. If she went to a regular school or an independent study course like me.

Which is why we've got such a small group of students here. The independent course, I mean. A few of them did it to graduate high school early, but a majority of them, myself included, are here because we were not cut out for regular school.

Since we're the throwaways, we're also wearing cheap, borrowed cap and gowns that make my arms itch. Or maybe that has to do with the fact I've got a hundred pairs of eyes on me.

I want to crawl out of my own skin. Peel it off and run screaming from the room.

I keep scanning the crowd, over the tops of heads, looking for Maggie. I don't see her but I know she's out there somewhere. I left the house this morning after she waved me off and told me to get out of her hair so she could make herself look presentable for the ceremony. And despite her clipped tone, I knew she was pleased. After all, we've spent the last three years, since she took me in as her foster kid, not knowing if I'd make it to this. I wouldn't have if it weren't for her.

"Vincent Hazelwood," calls the announcer.

The guy standing next to me shoves an elbow into my ribs so I'll step forward. I can't walk across this small stage with all these eyes on me. No way. I flunked subjects because I refused to get up in front of the class to give reports or participate in group activities.

But Maggie is out there. And I've let her down so much. It would be nice to make her proud with my attempt to be normal, even just this once.

SUICIDE WATCH

    Legs wobbling, I shamble to the lady at the mic and take the diploma she offers me. Even shake her hand and manage a tight-lipped smile, which I offer to the crowd. See, I can do something without screwing it up. Though I don't say *thank you* before hurrying off the stage because I'm about three seconds from either bursting into tears, or hurling on her nice shoes.

    In the adjoining room, I claw off the scratchy gown and toss the cap aside, clutching the diploma tight. Maybe it's nothing special, maybe it's not even like a *real* diploma from a *real* high school (I never asked if they were the same) but, damn it, it's mine and I worked hard for it. All I want to do is get out of here and find Maggie and show it to her. Maybe she will take me for something nice to eat. Maybe she will even give me a hug. She doesn't do that often.

    They're on the T names when I step back into the main room and start squirming my way through the tightly packed crowd. So many people for so few graduates all squeezed into a little rented auditorium like sardines. Yet even once I've made it to the far back near the double doors leading out, there's no sign of Maggie. She would've seen me get off stage and headed for the exit, right?

    I wait until the rest of the graduates are called. Until the kids I know vaguely by faces but not names have joined up with their families and move past me out the doors until there are just a handful left.

    A handful, me, and no Maggie.

    Maybe she's running late. That's what I tell myself as I head out to the parking lot, squinting, looking around for her ugly gold minivan. As quickly as I think it, I know it's unlikely. Maggie is a lot of things—distant, crass, cranky, overbearing—but she's never late.

    I fish my lock key and phone out of my pocket as I head for my bike. I've got three missed calls from a number I don't recognize, and a voicemail. I halt beside my bike, heart thumping wildly. I can feel it in my fingertips, my toes, my ears. That number doesn't have to mean anything. They're just numbers. Maybe even a wrong number. I get people calling all the time asking for someone who isn't me. Nobody calls me except Maggie. I unlock the bike and swing onto it, and let the voicemail play.

"Hi, this is Debra. I'm calling from Shire Hospital for Vincent Hazelwood. If you could please give me a call back..."

What does that mean? Why would the hospital be calling?

Unless—unless. Maggie fell. Broke a leg, a wrist, a hip. She's a tough old dame, but she's got the bones of a bird like anyone her age would. I'll try not to be mad when I see her. I guess a broken bone is a good enough reason for having missed out on my important day. Though I wish I would've known so I could spare myself the agony of walking across that stage.

I don't call Debra back. The hospital's between here and home, so I'll head over there. If Maggie broke something, she'll need me to drive anyway. Right? Right.

I've never really been in a hospital before. Never needed to. So I turn in circles until someone points me to a nurse's station and I tell them my name, and that I'm looking for Debra. They send me to another nurse's station down the hall where I find a short, pudgy lady with graying hair, and a name tag. Debra. I stand in front of her desk and stare at her until she looks up.

"Oh, I didn't even—I'm sorry. Can I help you?"

I hold up my phone, like that'll somehow answer anything. "You, uh. You called me."

A frown tugs at her face.

"I'm Vince Hazelwood," I say, then repeat, "You called me."

Debra's expression immediately smooths out.

Softens. "Oh, honey..." She pushes her chair back and stands, stepping around the desk to draw me off to one side, out of the hall. "I called about Maggie Atkins. You're her...?"

"Foster son." My voice wavers. Where the hell did that come from? I would have liked to say *I'm her real son and she's my mom, where is she?* Except Maggie never adopted me officially. I wouldn't let her. "What'd she do, trip carrying laundry into the house? Fall in the shower?"

The look she's giving me...I don't like it. Makes my insides twist all up.

"She had a heart-attack, sweetheart," Debra says.

I squint at her, not understanding. "Okay."

"Earlier this afternoon. A neighbor was there. But by the time the ambulance arrived, there was nothing they could do."

She strokes my arm but I don't really feel it. Kind of numb all over, actually. All I can think to say is, "Women don't die from heart-attacks."

"They..." Debra purses her lips. "What makes you think that?"

I stare at her because I don't have an answer. It seems true. Statistics or something, isn't it? Maybe if I say it enough, think it enough, it'll *be* true.

But it's not.

At the end of the day, I'm still peddling the four miles home where Maggie left chicken thawing on the counter for dinner and the book she was reading is open on the table. I wonder if it was a good book. I wonder if she would be disappointed she didn't get to finish it.

I pick up the book and throw it across the room. The sound it makes hitting the far wall isn't as satisfying as I hoped it would be.

I think I should be doing something. Maybe calling people to tell them what's happened. Maggie has a few friends whose numbers are listed in a rolodex in the kitchen, but I'm willing to bet if our next-door neighbor, Penny, was here when it happened, everyone in town knows by now. Maggie doesn't have any family; she had a son who died in a war at some point, but otherwise it was just me and her.

It was one of the only things we had in common: we were all alone in the world.

Nobody wanted me. Not until Maggie.

The only person who ever gave me a real chance is dead, and all I can think is how disappointed I am she didn't see me graduate.

Something is wrong in my head.

I tear up my diploma. It's paper. Proof I was able to memorize some facts and copy them onto a few tests. Proof I did something everyone else does. It's not proof that I am special. I sit on the couch late into the night, thinking about Maggie. Thinking about loneliness and hospitals and useless papers that mean nothing at all to anyone once we're dead.

And I think maybe Jessica had the right idea all along.

SUICIDE WATCH

CHAPTER 2

I made my only friend when I was thirteen. Corey Larson was as much of a loner as I was, except where I sort of took it quietly, she was loud and in-your-face. We got on well and spent our weekends in front of the TV watching any movie where people died or blew things up. We trolled cemeteries at night. Her parents hated me.

Then I turned fifteen. I was getting into no less than three fights a month at school. My grades sucked so the kids thought I was stupid. I was quiet, moody, and kept to myself, so they thought I was stuck-up. I never had a girlfriend, so they thought I was gay.

Which I am, but that's not the point.

My foster family was more than ready to pass me on to someone else. Like clockwork. I'd been to five different homes by that point. Maggie took me in, but her place was six hours north.

Six hours was a huge distance for kids our age. I saw Corey twice in that first year, once in the second, and not a single time within the last twelve months. She's changed. Blossomed into this pretty, bubbly girl who attracts attention everywhere she goes and I guess...

I don't know. Guess she moved along, too. Outgrew me.

But Corey is my only option to talk to someone about Maggie. If I don't, I think I'm going to explode. Or throw myself out a window.

(Or off a bridge.)

The last few times I tried to call her, she either didn't answer or was quick to say she had to go. I'm not up for handling that kind of rejection, so the next morning I email her instead. It takes me thirty minutes to type up a page-long letter. Another thirty to cut out all but a few lines and

SUICIDE WATCH

make the words fit together right. To make sense of them.

> **From:** Vincent H <herecomesthesun@beemail.com>
>
> **To:** Corey Larson <larsonyyy@beemail.com>
>
> **Subject:** Hi
>
> Hey, how goes it? I miss you.
>
> Today I graduated high school and Maggie died of a heart attack. It would be nice to catch up. Give me a call.
>
> Love,
>
> Vinny

    Maybe she'll call. Maybe she won't. She didn't reply to my last four emails.
    But she is all I have.
    The only other person I speak to on any sort of regular basis is Penny-the-obnoxious-neighbor. Even though she was with Maggie when she died, she hasn't stopped by all day. Probably expecting me to crawl over there, hysterical, needing her sympathy. She's that sort of person. Likes feeling needed and useful and all that. I wonder how useful and needed she'd feel if she finally came over and found me hanging from the rafters in the garage. Or passed out on the kitchen floor after downing a bottle of pills.
    She probably wouldn't care.
    Rather than check my email every three minutes to see if she replies, I find Maggie's keys on the counter, get into her van (still smells like her perfume) and drive. Other than my morning jogs, there is only one place I ever go by choice: the city animal shelter.
    They've just opened when I show up. Volunteers in red shirts mingle around, talking with families about potential pet adoptions. I recognize faces here and there. If

anyone ever remembers me, they never say anything despite that I've been coming here several times a month for the last two years.

It's been kind of therapeutic, actually. Seeing the animals. Sitting in silence with something as lonely as I am and knowing they understand on this base, instinctive level that no one else does.

I head straight for the dog kennels. Cats are just fine, but they're in their own rooms with glass walls so I can't reach in and pet them without asking an employee to let me in. Then they might think I actually plan on adopting something, taking it home with me, and I would have to explain to them that I can't even take care of myself and no one in their right mind would leave me in charge of a living creature.

The kennels are loud, filled with the steady stream of barking. I never go for the barking dogs. I seek out the quietest, saddest-looking dog I can find. One that probably won't be here when I come back, because no one wanting it is what got it to the shelter in the first place, and no one wanting it is what gets it brought into the back room and killed.

The dog of the day is a Rottweiler mix named Bella. The fur around her muzzle is starting to gray, and she has trouble standing because of her hips. No one will adopt her because she's old and imperfect. I sit in front of her kennel, curling my fingers through the chain link, until she's relaxed enough with my presence to hobble over and investigate.

Corey used to ask me why I did this. *It's too fucking sad. Why would you spend your free time with dogs you know are going to die?* I couldn't explain it to her then, and I can't explain it to myself even now. Just that being here, as sad as it is, is comforting to me in a way most other things aren't.

Besides, everything dies.

I sit with Bella for two hours, stroking her head when she leans it against the fence with a heavy sigh. When I leave, I tell her I'm sorry and that I'll miss her. I never forget their names.

For the next three days, I do a lot of wandering around the house and not sleeping, blasting Beatles CDs at volumes that would have given Maggie a heart attack. (Ha.) I want to cry. Crying would be a normal reaction to this, to losing someone who was more family to me than anyone else ever has been. Being a wreck would be better than this: feeling nothing and everything all at once and physically unable to react to any of it.

Penny finally makes an appearance on the third day, but only long enough to tell me how upset she is to have lost such a good friend, and to ask when the funeral is. I stare at her blankly.

She frowns. "You *are* planning the funeral, aren't you?"

"Of course," I say, although I'm not. What would I know about planning funerals?

When the phone rings later, I throw myself at it and answer breathlessly, hoping for Corey. The person on the other end is most notably more male than Corey.

"*Vincent? Is that you? It's Harold.*"

I pause, running the name through the tattered rolodex that is my brain. "Oh."

"*Maggie's attorney.*"

"Uh huh," I say, because he's stupid if he thinks I don't know that. He's worked for Maggie for years, long before I came along. Even if I've only met him a handful of times in passing, I've heard her on the phone with him and they've gone out to lunch multiple times.

"*I'm so, so sorry for your loss, kiddo. I know it's a rough time right now, but can I swing by tonight and go over some paperwork with you?*"

What in the world does Maggie's lawyer want with me? But I say yeah, sure, and hang up, and later I wonder if he's coming to tell me something about the house. Obviously without Maggie here, no one is paying the mortgage or utilities, and I don't have a way to do it. Do I have to leave? Where do I go? I just finished high school, for crying out loud; I don't even have a job. I wouldn't know the first thing about getting one.

By the time Harold shows up in his crisp suit and slicked-back, graying hair, I've worked myself up into a stage of debilitating panic, and there's no time to take my medication to mellow myself out. Where's a paper bag when I need one?

Harold doesn't look at all concerned as he sets his briefcase down and takes a seat. Well, okay, maybe he looks sad. He and Maggie have known each other for like twenty years. But he called me *kiddo* and he's coming to throw me out of my home, so I refuse to feel too sorry for him.

Harold folds his hands on the table. I sit across from him. He's in Maggie's seat. I can't think of a nice way to tell him to move.

"How are you holding up, Vincent?"

Shrug. "Fine."

His eyes soften in that sympathetic *you poor thing* look the nurses at the hospital gave me. "I'll try not to drag this on too long..."

"I don't want to leave," I blurt. My hands are trembling a samba in my lap.

Harold stops in the middle of unclasping his briefcase. "What?"

"The house. I don't want to leave the house. Do I have to?"

"Vincent..." A soft sigh puffs past his lips. "Well, let me explain first. The situation isn't that bad."

The tightness in my chest uncoils. Just a little. "Okay."

"Maggie was pretty upside down on this place. I don't really think she intended to keep it much longer." He shuffles through a few papers and pulls some out. "This is her last will and testament. She had me update it last winter. Do you want to read it?"

He passes them over to me without waiting for an answer. The will looks depressingly like some kind of contract. I don't really see the words or understand them. Except my name. I see my name in there. A lot, actually.

"I don't understand."

"The bank will be taking the house back. I can get you sixty days before you have to be out." He slowly slides the papers out of my hands.

Out. Out on the streets? What's good about that?

"You won't have the house, but you'll have the rest of her assets. I won't lie; it isn't a lot, but it should keep you more than comfortable until you can get back on your feet."

"Assets," I repeat. "So...what, like money?"

He smiles crookedly and tips his head. "That's the gist of it, yes. Has the funeral home contacted you?" When I shake my head, he continues, "Maggie had a pre-plan. That is, she had everything for her funeral paid for ahead of time. You won't have to worry about any of that. I can take care of whatever paperwork they need if you aren't feeling up for it."

I'm relieved because I don't know what I would've done otherwise. But along the same vein, I wonder—did Maggie make all these plans because she expected she would die? Because she didn't trust me to take care of it? I guess I can't blame her. I duck my head into a nod.

Harold places a hand on my arm, mistaking my distress for grief. "Everything will be okay, kiddo."

What does he know? Maggie's dead. I have to leave my home. I'll have money to last me for awhile, but then what? Maggie wanted me to go to college, but I can't do it without her here. Why would I? It was *her* dream. It was what *she* wanted for me.

If she's not here to want it, I don't know how to want it for myself.

When Harold leaves, I try to distract myself by making something to eat. I haven't eaten much, and Maggie's niggling voice in the back of my brain tells me I should. Except I don't know how to cook. Maggie always did it. I try to make a dinner like she would, with meat and corn and applesauce—skipping the potatoes because I'm nowhere near confident enough to try.

A packet of paperwork Harold left sits on the dining table, taunting me. A reminder that the countdown has started. X-days until I can say goodbye to my home.

The meat is burnt to a crisp. The corn is watery.

I can't get the lid to the applesauce off. The jar ends up on the ground and I'm kneeling there amongst the broken pieces, hysterical, in tears. I'm crying over applesauce, but none of the things that matter.

What is wrong with me?

SUICIDE WATCH

CHAPTER 3

Corey hasn't written back.

I spend my evenings staring at the phone, contemplating calling just to hear someone's voice who isn't Harold or Penny. I wonder if she'll call while I'm out of the house for the funeral.

It's the first time I've stepped outside since graduation other than to go to the shelter. I shower and scrub myself clean, comb my typically messy curls back as best as I can and put on the black slacks and white button-up shirt Maggie bought for me to wear to a Christmas event last year. I hate it, but she liked it, and today will be the last day I can do anything for her.

Harold offered to drive me to the service, but I refused. I want an easy way out if I need to leave, and being tethered to someone for a ride home won't help.

I should probably cut Harold a break. He's only trying to help, and I think he's a genuinely nice guy concerned for my well-being. But he's not a friend, and he's not family. I don't even know what I'm feeling, so how am I supposed to answer his worried glances and questions with anything other than a shrug and *I'm fine.*

I *am* fine. I'm dandy.

I'm just great.

Say it enough and I might start to believe it.

I wonder if Jessica the Jumper said that to people the day she leapt off the bridge. *I'm great, thanks for asking.* I wonder if people realized how un-fine she really was.

Maggie's funeral is simple. She didn't go all-out for a fancy casket or an elaborate ceremony. It's just like her: practical. I sit far in the back, wondering who all these people are. Some I think must be from her Friday night bingo group. Others are neighbors. A couple people approach me after the service with sympathetic looks, touching my face and arms while I try to shy away. I didn't want to go up front where Maggie's casket is open. But while everyone mingles and murmurs amongst themselves, Penny waddles over and links her arm with mine, and I don't have much of a choice but to go along unless I want to make a scene.

The casket is made out of a dark, reddish wood, polished to where I can see myself in it. Inside is lined with blue satin, matching the dress she's wearing. She loved that dress. Maggie's gray hair is all done up like she always wore it. Though something about her face, her closed eyes, thin mouth, sharp features...it looks all wrong. Not like her at all.

I think Penny is waiting for something from me. Some massive melt-down, tears, hysterics. I don't know. Honestly, I'm kind of waiting for it, too, being the world's biggest crybaby, after all. After the applesauce incident, I spent three hours sobbing and unable to stop. Yet there are no tears now, when there should be.

Penny strokes my arm. "It's time to say goodbye, Vince."

I frown at Maggie.

She looks like clay.

That's what it is. Like someone made a clay replica of Maggie's head. I could reach down and smudge away a wrinkle, leave my fingerprint in her skin. "I can't say goodbye."

"I know it's hard, sweetheart, but—"

"Of course it's hard. She's *dead*. How do you say goodbye to someone who's already dead?" I pull my arm out of her grasp. "Saying goodbye to dead people doesn't mean a thing. They can't hear you."

By the stricken look on her face, you would think I'd slapped her. Nevermind that I didn't even raise my voice. It's still flat and easy, because I can't find it in me to get worked up about this. She's dead, and it sucks. It *really fucking sucks* but what am I supposed to do?

I could handle being sad.

Whatever *this* is, this in-between phase of feeling and not, I hate it.

I leave before Penny — or Harold, or anyone else — can give me anymore words of wisdom about *letting go* and how Maggie is in a better place. I go home and claw off my stupid formal clothes and mess up my hair, and I think about how I have to pack everything in the house to either take it with me or sell it. I'm going to have to look through everything *Maggie* in this place before I'm kicked out in less than two months.

What then? I can get an apartment of my own, sure. A job. Something. What's the point? I find it hard to think of a point to any of this. I think if there were one person who cared, *just one*, I could find a reason to give a damn.

I pick up the phone and call Corey.

Through the house phone instead of my cell, because she won't recognize the number and maybe she'll answer instead of sending me to voicemail. It rings once, twice, and her voice comes alive on the line, cheerful and warm.

"*Hello!*"

If there's anyone I want to break down to, it's her. I think I could, would, if I could see her face to face. "Hey, it's me."

A pause. "*Hey, Vinny. What's going on?*"

She didn't read my email. So maybe she wasn't avoiding me and maybe this is all some stupid misunderstanding and I'm just...being needy. Too clingy. Expecting too much. "You know. Stuff. Look, I was wondering if maybe I could come down for a visit? I've got the van, so..."

Another long pause wherein I make out muffled voices and laughter in the background. She's out with friends. A new boyfriend, maybe. I try to give my hands something to do by opening a cupboard and pulling out cups to pack. Small, porcelain things. Very delicate. Maggie used them for tea.

"*Look... I'm not sure that's a great idea.*"

My insides curl and tighten with a million painful little reminders that I exist more than I want to. "I emailed you the other day. I could really..." Deep breath. Gripping a cup tighter than I should. "I could really stand to see you right now, you know? It's been over a year. "And I need you. I need you, I need you, I need you.

I need something. Someone.

"*Exactly, Vin, it's been over a year. I mean, it was great when you lived down here, right? It was cool. But...maybe ,you know, you should get some friends up there?*"

I look down at the cup in my hands, and let it fall to the floor where it breaks into a hundred tiny pieces.

Just like that. She's moved on. No more room for me, right?

Forgotten.

The second falls, shatters.

Like every foster home who has shuffled me off with excuses. Like my parents did when they decided they couldn't keep me. Corey was the one person I held out hope for that wouldn't do this to me, and I think of what Maggie used to say, *Humans are imperfect. That's all there is to it.* And, boy, was she right. I'm the most imperfect of them all.

"*Vin?*"

Another cup bites the dust.

"Yeah. I'm here."

"*I should go... I'm sorry.*" The funny thing is, she sounds like she means it.

"Sure." I hear her sit there a moment longer, as though debating. Feeling bad, maybe. When I don't say anything further, Corey says "*Good bye, Vinny,*" and hangs up.

One more cup. The last of the four-piece set. The sound it makes is satisfying for nothing more than a fleeting second.

I wonder if Corey will read my email. I hope she doesn't. I've never wanted to be in anyone's way — most of all, Corey's — and if leaving me behind is what she wants, then I —

What does it matter anymore?

Around midnight, I pull on sweat-pants and a t-shirt and go out for a run. Instead of my usual route passing by the Woodshire bridge, I cross it, and come to a halt at the spot I saw Jessica the Jumper on Christmas Eve.

I remember her serene face and wonder what would have happened if I'd stopped her. If I had run over, grabbed the back of her plaid coat and dragged her away from the ledge. Would she have been grateful or would she have hated me for getting in the way? Because when someone is so close to the edge that plummeting seventy miles per hour to your death becomes a better option than sloshing through one more day, you have to wonder if they *really* want to be saved.

I grip the railing. The metal is so cold it almost burns my palms. After a moment, I start to swing a leg over it.

Nobody will miss me, Jessica had said.

Nobody will miss me, either.

But...

I miss her, don't I? I wanted to know more about her. I wanted to know what made her sound as lonely as I am.

I pull back from the railing and step away. My heart is racing.

Even though I feel like I'm going to be sick, I manage to jog home without the added embarrassment. The second I'm through the door and in my room, I turn on music from my computer and crank up the volume as though the lonely lyrics of John Lennon will somehow drown out my

SUICIDE WATCH

thoughts.

I pull open an internet browser and, after staring at it for awhile, I type in the only thing I can think of.

What's it like to die?

The number of results that pop up is overwhelming. I could read twenty pages worth and not even put a dent in it. No one's answer is quite the same. Some say it's peaceful. Like falling asleep. 'Suffocating, terrifying,' others say. 'The feeling of being dragged out of your own body...'

Nestled amongst the many windows I've opened of blog entries, spiritual websites, and new-age crap, is a site I must've clicked on by accident. There's nothing remarkable about its front page. No explanation as to what it is. Only a request to login, and a black and white logo that reads:

Suicide Watch

I click on the image. At the top is a short blurb:

Welcome to Suicide Watch. This site is not for the faint of heart. Only the serious need apply. Please think carefully prior to filling out the registration form and submitting.

I'm wondering what they mean by *only the serious* when I scroll down to the registration questions. Name, email address, city and state...

My heart lodges in my throat. This? This is some kind of scam. It has to be. It's some bleeding-heart group that reels in potential suicide victims and tries to fix them. They nab all the depressed high school kids who want to down a bottle of pills and contact their parents, I'll bet. Except they aren't asking for much info. Not even a last name. Just a first name, vague location, and an email address.

There have to be twenty guys named Vincent in Hillsdale, on this side of the bridge alone. Besides, who would they call? The only person in my life who would have cared will be six feet under by the time the sun goes down.

Before I realize it, I've filled in the registration form. Why? Am I seriously, *honestly* considering this? I don't know, but I think I might be. I tried explaining to Maggie once that either I feel nothing at all, or everything at once. There is no happy medium with me, and it makes everything so hard. I don't know what I'm doing. I don't know that I want to die. The entire idea seems so overdramatic and stupid. And maybe it isn't that I want to die, exactly.

	But living is getting to be far too lonely.

SUICIDE WATCH

CHAPTER 4

Through my night of non-sleep, I slowly and mechanically begin to pack. There are a ton of spare boxes in the garage Maggie insisted we might need someday—and how right she was—so I drag them into the living room.

All of this stuff? Harold said it's mine now. But I wouldn't know what to do with any of it. I don't want to look at it. These old lamps and coasters and throw pillows and rugs and Maggie, Maggie, Maggie. Even though I lived here, I was always very conscious that this was *her* home and not mine. I never left my things lying around outside the safety of my own little room. It was a way of defending myself, I guess. So I wasn't constantly reminding her I was there, and therefore she was less likely to want to get rid of me.

Within a few hours I've packed up most of the living room: movies, old records and CDs, artwork on the walls, lamps, candles. I shove them into boxes labeled for the Good Will. Someone might as well get use out of them. I'm at a loss what to do with the furniture, until the idea dawns on me to take pictures and post them on Craigslist. So that's what I do.

When I sit back at the computer to upload the photos, there's an email waiting for me.

SUICIDE WATCH

> **From:** HARBINGER <admin@yoursuicidewatch.com>
>
> **To:** Vincent H. <herecomesthesun@beemail.com>
>
> **Subject:** Membership Confirmation (Do Not Reply)
>
> Thank you for joining SW. Please click the link below, choose your username, and introduce yourself in the forums.
>
> Sincerely,
>
> Harbinger (Site Admin)

Any anxiety I had last night about the site being a scam has ebbed away. Maybe because I'm so exhausted that my emotions have numbed more than they usually are. After some thought and inspiration from the Beatles, I set my username as *NowhereMan*.

The site itself isn't anything impressive. The layout is basic and unremarkable. The links across the top read Videos, Stories, Pictures, and Forum. My cursor lingers over the first three tabs before I choose pictures. The thumbnails that load are a little too small to really make out, so I click on the first one. It's a terrible quality pic, maybe taken with a webcam, of a girl sleeping in her bed.

Sleeping, or —

Luxwood87, SW member, memorializes her passing with one last photo, reads the caption.

My heart stops.

Her face is what gets me. She has on that same slack, calm expression Jessica wore. In death, she feels no pain, no sorrow, no loneliness. And she set her webcam up so the people on this website could witness it.

I spend the next hour skimming through pictures, some more gruesome than others. Many are webcam photos taken from a live feed posted under the videos section, but I haven't brought myself to watch any of those yet. Seeing pictures is one thing. Watching it happen is another. The pictures capture a mere flicker in time, usually after the person is already dead. Even then, some of them I have to click out of quickly or risk losing the Cheerios I had for breakfast. It's the gunshot ones that get me the most. People who put a bullet in their heads. At the bottom of one reads: *AscottPrice, long-time SW member, has left this world to join his wife in the next. Photo taken by site admin, Harbinger.*

My blood runs cold. Why would someone else take a picture of this? Or rather, why would someone sit back and *watch*?

(Right. Like I watched Jessica?)

I decide I'm done with the pictures and click over to the forum instead, not really knowing what to expect. A few seconds of skimming the page tells me all I need to know. This site really, truly is dedicated to people wanting to die.

The sub forums cover methods of suicide—the least painful, the most creative, the fastest—to group discussions about what comes after death, and even places to discuss movies and music or whatever the hell else you want. Like it was any old forum for people to mingle and share interests. With the number of posts as recent as seconds ago, it's obvious the place gets some good buzz and stays fairly busy. Some members have countdown timers in their signatures.

49 days, 8 hours, 3 minutes.

I shiver.

I still don't know what I think about this. Any of this. If this is what I want, if this is what I need. But I'm morbidly curious and I want to figure it out. Knowing there are other people out there who *get it*, who have the same questions I do, makes the whole idea seem less ridiculous.

There's a new members sub forum, but I stare at the posting screen forever and can't think of anything to say beyond *hi*. I don't want to write about myself and send it out there into empty space. What if nobody responds? Instead I wander through other postings.

Soon I'm engrossed in stories of what led these people to this website. Their losses, the things they've had taken from them. I see the terminally ill, the clinically depressed, the kids bullied at school, the gays turned away by their families, the husbands and wives who lost everything when their spouses left them for the new, improved model.

I find the lonely ones, like me.

The people who haven't lost anything, because they never had it to begin with.

The usernames have cities and states listed under them, and I find a girl nicknamed Casper who lives in Walnut Glen, about forty-five minutes away from Hillsdale. Her post talks about her 'treatments,' an art gallery her parents took her to, and her favorite TV shows. And I'm not sure what to reply because these other commenters obviously know this girl to talk to her like they do. I feel kind of awkward, but I finally respond:

NowhereMan (Hillsdale, CA)

My city has a pretty neat gallery. Next month they're doing a feature on graffiti artists.

Nevermind that I've never actually been to the downtown art gallery, and that I had to look it up to see what sort of events they're holding. It's stupid, right? Going through that kind of effort.

That's how it's always been, though. Going out of my way to have something in common with someone. When I first met Corey she was nice and all, but I got her to hang out with me outside of school by pretending to be interested in her favorite female rock band, *Calamity Kitty*, who was in town doing an autograph session to mark the release of a new album. I never did admit to her how much I *hated* that band.

Twenty minutes later, a response. Not on the original post, but sent directly via private message.

Casper: Looks kind of cool. You going?

A connection. A link. Someone who read something I wrote and thought it worthy of a response, no matter how brief.

NowhereMan: Hadn't really thought about it. I don't get out much.

Which was true even before Maggie died. I preferred staying at home in my room, listening to music or playing my video games. Drove Maggie nuts.

Casper: Neither do I. So what's your damage?

What *is* my damage?

NowhereMan: I don't know. What treatments are you doing? Are you sick?

Casper: Cancer. Various treatments. Gets old after awhile.

The two of us message back and forth for the better part of two hours. I never ask her name and she doesn't ask mine, but I learn she's been sick for awhile and the treatments she's undergoing aren't working too well. I would feel sorry for her, but I get the impression pity is the last thing she wants.

Eventually, she says she has to go and she'll 'catch

me around.' That's a good thing. Isn't it a good thing? Casper talks with the distant sort of aura that suggests she isn't big on making close friends. Then again, I've heard that said about me before, too.

Just as I'm about to close out the browser, another private message pops onto the screen. This one isn't from Casper, but someone with the username RoxWell. The subject line says nothing more than *hi*. Not sure if I should be weirded out someone is PM'ing me when I've made a whole one post on the site, but okay.

In the message are the first few lines of the Beatles' *Nowhere Man*. The sight of it makes my insides flip-flop. I know the words. Of course I do. And it's probably stupid to think no one else would get the reference of my username, but the fact that someone does makes me feel warm all over.

I respond with the next few lines, then click send and wait.

CHAPTER 5

Over the next few weeks, the house begins to empty. In my online for-sale ads, I didn't know what kind of prices to list for any of Maggie's stuff, so I put *best offer*. Pretty sure some of the offers I'm getting aren't at all anyone's best but, really, I just want this shit out of the house.

It hurts to look at how little a person's possessions mean when they're gone. I know I wanted to feel something, but now I'm not so sure. Grass is always greener on the other side or something.

A newlywed pair buys the dining set, and a couple of guys take the couches and coffee table. Maggie's bedroom furniture is trickier, because the bed has to be disassembled before anyone can get it out of there and I won't help. I can't stomach being in her room. Instead I stand in the hallway and listen to a father and son taking the bed to pieces, chatting away. I'm trying not to imagine Maggie's permanent satin-lined bed at the cemetery when my cell rings. No one is paying me any attention so I slip downstairs to answer it, knowing it's Corey by the ringtone.

"Hello."

"*I just read your email. Vinny, oh my god, I'm so, so sorry.*"

I roll my gaze to the ceiling. How long has it been since I sent that? And she's just now sitting down to read it? Either that, or she read it ages ago and couldn't think of what to say. "Yeah, well, you know."

"*I had no idea when I talked to you — are you all right? Do you need anything?*"

What a funny moment for a flashback.

School. Hallways. Guys slamming me into the lockers and calling me a fag.

Corey getting between us and screaming in his face,

before turning to me. *Are you all right, are you okay, Vinny, I'm so sorry...*

Then I think about Harold, calling every few days to give me an update on whatever paperwork he's doing and getting me the money he says I have coming. I think about Casper, who I've talked to nearly every day online through Suicide Watch for the last three weeks, and the bridge, and Jessica, and the dogs at the shelter who will be dead soon, and RoxWell who messages me with random lyrics from Beatles songs, but never says anything otherwise.

Amidst all that, I try to figure out if I need anything from Corey, and I come up blank.

"I could've used a friend," I say. "But it's too late for that."

"*Vinny* – "

"You were right, you know? We've got nothing in common anymore. You've moved on. So don't worry about it now just because you're feeling guilty. I've gotta go." I don't wait for her to answer before hanging up. She doesn't call back.

This is how you get rid of someone before they can get rid of you.

The guys upstairs finish with Maggie's bed and drag it out to their truck. They end up buying her dresser, too, as an afterthought. Once they leave, the house is now fifty percent empty, and my heart hurts.

There's a message from Casper waiting for me when I sign onto the forums. The last one I'd sent her before she signed off last night had been:

> **NowhereMan:** So I have kind of a weird question. I was looking through the pictures and videos and stuff, and you know, the guy who runs the site is labeled as having taken some of them. What's up with that?

It was a trend I noticed. People that lived in or around Harbinger's city. He seems nice enough from his forum posts, though I've never spoken to him directly.

It's awhile before Casper responds to me.

Casper: What's your email address?

A weird question in response to my weird question. Okay. Casper and I have talked about everything under the sun the last two weeks. Art, music, movies, celebrity gossip, and other stupid crap, but never anything of depth. Never anything that matters. I don't know if it's because I'm holding her at arm's length, or she's doing it with me, but there's a wall between us and neither of us seem to mind. Regardless, I send her my address and a few minutes later, my regular email pings.

From: C Harms <fangtastic@kooncast.net>

To: <herecomesthesun@beemail.com>

Subject: Stuff

Harbinger is very active in the site. He's been known to go to some members' houses when they're ready to off themselves and record it for them. Sorta like their last message to the world or something. Freaky, huh?

For a second, I wonder if Casper actually is her real name. Probably shouldn't ask. There's a reason people use fake names on the internet, especially through a site like this. We all like our anonyminity. And yet, I sort of forget she'll see my real first name when I write her back. I don't think it bothers me. It's just a name.

From: Vincent H. <herecomesthesun@beemail.com>

To: C Harms <fangtastic@kooncast.net>

Subject: RE: Stuff

Freaky is a word for it. I was thinking illegal. And kind of sad.

She writes back:

From: C Harms <fangtastic@kooncast.net>

To: Vincent H. <herecomesthesun@beemail.com>

Subject: RE: Stuff

Death shouldn't be a sad thing. I mean, it is, it can be. But, like, not always. It's sad when people die unexpectedly and they didn't want to. I think it stops being sad when we're able to take matters into our own hands and control it.

I chew on that for awhile. She's sick, I remember. And maybe she won't survive and maybe that's why she's involved in SW.

Me: Are you really going to kill yourself?

Her: Are you?

Me: I don't know. Some days I think I'm okay. Other days, not so much. I saw a girl jump off a bridge last Christmas. One right by my house. Every time I pass that bridge, I think about jumping.

Her: So why haven't you?

Me: It used to be 'cause of my foster mom. I thought if I had one person in my life, I shouldn't make them sad by going away.

Her: And she's the one who died, right? So...what are you gonna do now?

Me: That's why I joined SW. Trying to figure that out. You never answered my question. Are you going to do it?

There's a stagnant, fifteen minute pause before she replies:

I'll do it before the cancer does.

SUICIDE WATCH

July

SUICIDE WATCH

CHAPTER 6

From: Vincent H. <herecomesthesun@beemail.com>

To: RoxWell <adayinthelife@beemail.com>

Subject: one of those days.

I talked to my foster mom's lawyer again last night. He calls a lot to see how I'm doing. It's weird. You'd think Penny, our neighbor, would check in on me more because she knows me a lot better, but she doesn't.

Maybe she's mad about the funeral. I told her I couldn't say goodbye to Maggie because she's dead. Doesn't that make sense? How do you say goodbye to someone who can't hear you?

I wish someone would have just said, "Hey, sorry, this blows." At least it would have felt sincere. At least I could have agreed with that, rather than saying she's in a better place.

If she's in a better place, why are the rest of us trying so hard to stay where we are?

SUICIDE WATCH

CHAPTER 7

Harold presents me with a check for more money than I've ever seen in my life. Granted, like he said, it's only enough to let me live comfortably for awhile. A few months. Maybe close to a year, if I'm careful. I don't even know if I'll be around that long. A year seems like a lifetime. Harold asks if I need help looking for a new apartment and even though I do, I say no thanks.

I still have a month left, so I'll put it off a bit longer.

Corey emailed me a few nights ago, asking how I was, if I needed to talk. Begging me to call her. Part of me wanted to throw myself at the computer screen and tell her yes—*yes*, I want to talk. I have so much to say and all these thoughts and feelings swirling around my brain and in my chest like itching ants, and I could tear my heart open just to get it all out.

I want to, but I don't. She made her stance clear. She's moved on, and I refuse to be anybody's charity case. I deleted her mail without responding.

Besides, I have Casper and to a lesser degree, RoxWell, who still never writes me anything but song lyrics. But it's sort of our weird thing now. I've started sending him messages, telling him about my day. He'll respond with lyrics from a song that says what he's trying to get across. He's had to stray from Beatles songs to get the right effect, but that's okay.

Casper is something else. She's brass and blunt, and tells me I'm over-sensitive so there are a lot of things I don't tell her. Sometimes she has bad days and goes off on rants about stupid things, but most of the time...I don't know. I think she's just tired. She's got these parents who love her to pieces and it's killing her right along with the cancer.

I need to get out of this house, she writes me tonight.

SUICIDE WATCH

Let's go do something. Go somewhere. Weren't you saying there was an art show where you're at?

That was so long ago I almost don't remember. I still have the page bookmarked, so I forward her the link. Then it dawns on me what she said.

She wants to go do something.

With *me*.

In person.

Before I can think of an excuse to not go, she writes: *Sounds good. I can take the light-rail downtown and you can meet me?*

My heart races. What a terrible idea and why on earth would she think of it?

Me: You don't want to meet me.

Her: Why not? Are you ugly?

Me: I don't know...

Her: It was a joke.

Me: Oh.

Her: There's a route that runs at 10:35 which would put me there around noon. Cool?

I have no other excuse. I am excuseless. What I gave her was the best I had. She's going to meet me, and she's going to realize I don't know how to filter what I say and I'm stupid and can hardly walk and chew gum at the same time. More than that, she'll realize how utterly, totally uninteresting I am. But she'd tell me I'm being an idiot if I tried to explain that, so I tell her it's cool even though it's not, and I try to refrain from having a panic-attack.

I PM RoxWell, though I leave out the details.

NowhereMan: I'm doing something utterly terrifying this weekend. I'm hanging out with someone and what if this someone realizes I'm not worth hanging out with?

He doesn't write back until I'm getting ready for bed. For the first time there are no lyrics, but the message is short and to the point and I reread it a hundred times.

RoxWell: Don't worry so much. You are.

I get to the light-rail station at a quarter to noon. The trams run every thirty minutes, so the next one ought to be hers. I was so shook up with nerves I almost emailed Casper to tell her I was sick and had to cancel, until I realized what time it was. She would've already left the house to get here. Too late now.

In my medicine cabinet is a bottle of pills. Anxiety medication, prescribed awhile back by a psychiatrist Maggie talked me into seeing. I went once. Did not go back.

I take them only when I really, *really* need them, when I feel like my emotions are going to burst out of my chest like some tangible creature and eat me from the inside, out. I almost take them. Almost. But they have a bad habit of knocking me on my ass and I'm not sure that's what I want right now. After feeling so numb over Maggie's death, the panic is nearly a welcome sensation.

As the light-rail rumbles to a stop, it dawns on me I don't have a clue what Casper looks like. We've never exchanged pictures. Hell, I never even asked what her real name was. I don't know much of anything about her beyond her misery. And for as little as I know about her, she knows even less about me because she tends to do most of the talking.

Yet, the second she steps off the train, I recognize her.

Aside from the fact she's the only girl who stops and looks around like she's waiting for someone, there's just...something about her. She's small. Five-foot-four, if she's lucky, and she's got this shock of short blonde hair and a cherub face that makes me wonder just how old she is. She mentioned high school before so she can't be that young.

I take a few steps down the stairs. This is my last chance to back out. Of course, if I do it'll mean I can never show my face at SW again. Not that they'd miss me; my few occasional, lame responses and attempts and connecting to people in the forums aren't any more effective than my attempts to connect to people in real life.

Casper spots me and lifts a hand like I can't see her, and heads in my direction. When she's closer, I realize she's actually kind of pretty, even though there are dark circles under her eyes and she could use some meat on her bones. She has on striped leggings and mismatched clothes. Her small size emphasizes how little she weighs, and I wonder if that's some sort of result of her being sick, or if she's always been that way.

"Hey," she says.

I duck my head and stare at my shoes. "Hey."

"Glad to see you aren't secretly some forty-year-old sleaze waiting to take advantage of me in the back of a van."

"I do have a van," I say.

Her mouth twists into a crooked, wry grin. "So where are we going?"

I stare at her blankly.

"The art show? Hello?"

"Oh." Right. I hunch up my shoulders and gesture for her to follow. The gallery is only a few blocks away, and we're fortunate it hasn't gotten too hot outside yet. I hate summers. I miss the winter rain where everything smells clean and renewed, not reeking and struggling to stay alive beneath the onslaught of sun and global warming.

Along the way, I try to think of something to say. A

conversation starter. I'm honestly surprised she's not chatting my ear off; she can go on for pages through email. Maybe she's shyer in real life. "Um... How was the trip?"

She gives me a sidelong look and a raised eyebrow. "It was a trip."

"Your parents were cool with you coming all the way out here?"

"How could they not be when I didn't tell them?" She fusses with a barrette in her hair. I think it's Hello Kitty. "They don't let me go anywhere anymore."

I frown. "Because you're sick?"

"Because I'm sick," she confirms. "But if I'm gonna die anyway, I don't want to be stuck in my room for what time I've got left."

I imagine Casper's name in the forums, what it might look like with one of those timers beneath it in her signature. What would hers say, I wonder? Six months, seven months, ten years... I wonder what her diagnosis is. How much time the doctors gave her if the treatment doesn't start to work. But I don't know how to ask, so I don't.

We find the gallery. There are two people in line in front of us. Tickets are only five bucks a piece, but I pay for it anyway, seeing as she had to buy her ticket for the trip out here. Inside, we're reminded of the wonders of central air. No more sweat along the nape of my neck or making my shirt stick to my back.

We wander the halls where each mural stretches out. I try to imagine an artist buying all this sheetrock instead of regular canvases. They're huge. Taller than I am, some wider than my bedroom. Transportable walls pulled out of suburbia and placed inside the confines of a museum. They look out of place here. These are things I ought to see on the sides of abandoned buildings or along railway tracks. Something beautiful and bright to add charm to otherwise dirty and decaying things.

We linger in front of each painting, and Casper leans

in to read the placards about each artist aloud. I try to think of something profound or intelligent-sounding to say.

At a mural of a wide, snow-covered forest, I stop completely while Casper reads. The piece is haunting and eerie and empty, made moreso by the fact it's viewed as though through a thick sheet of glass, subtly warping the bare branches and making the dreary sky seem lonely.

I bite my lip, struggling for words. "It's kind of like...he's, you know..." Something witty, something smart. Nothing comes. Casper glances at me sidelong while I stutter and grasp blindly, before she grins.

"Dude, easy. It's just a picture."

My mouth snaps shut. I stare at the mural, face burning.

"Seriously," she says. "I'm not some fancy art person who tries picking apart the meaning of everything. If something's pretty, I like it. If something's not...I don't. I'm not even big on art."

"Then why did you ask to come to the gallery?"

"Like I said, I was really tired of being stuck at home."

"Oh." A pause. "Do you like this one?" It's an easier question. So much easier.

"I do." She shoves her hands into her pockets. "How about you?"

The tension slips out of me. "Yeah. Me, too."

"You know who'd like this kind of stuff?" she says, and meanders down the hall for the next mural. "RoxWell. You talk to him, right?"

By some miracle I manage not to trip over my own feet. "Uh—yeah. I mean, sort of. I guess. If you call what we do talking. You know him?"

"Know him? I'm the one who told him he should contact you." She casts a patient look at me over her shoulder. "He lives around here, too, you know."

My heart stutters in my chest and I bite my lip. So

did RoxWell know who I was talking about when I told him I was going out with someone? Does he think we're here on some kind of date? That would be stupid and even if it were true, I don't see why he'd care. "Yeah. He's just...not the talkative type, I guess."

"He's shy." After looking around, Casper leans up to gently brush her fingers over the painting, tracing lines of blue and gray. They don't have the kind of texture oil paintings do or anything, but she seems fascinated with the detail and fine lines the artist managed to get out of a can. "He's got a crappy home life, you know. His parents used to be real uppity, pushing him to be this perfect kid. Then his dad died and now his mom pretends he doesn't exist. But he loves art and music. Like, really loves it. He plays guitar. And sings."

"Is he good?"

"*I* think so, but he tells me I don't know enough about music to judge, so what do I know?" She shrugs and pulls her hand back, rubbing her fingers together. "If you two don't talk, 'exactly,' what do you do?"

I stare at the mural because it's easier not to blush when I do. "He...uh, he sends me song lyrics."

"He does that sometimes, yeah."

"All the time with me."

"I should introduce you two in person. Might get him to warm up to you some."

The idea of meeting this faceless person who likes all the right music makes me uneasy. I've talked to him—talked *at* him—plenty of times. Told him things without really meaning to, because he was a nameless, faceless void to throw my pain at.

"I don't know."

"I know how it is, Vince. I talk to this guy, Joey, who lives out East. He's got cancer, too. We kinda latched onto each other 'cause the support...it's nice. What've you got to lose? You're both miserable. Why not be miserable together?" Casper moves on. I follow.

I guess she's right. Misery does love company.

We spend two hours browsing the museum. I buy Casper and myself each a postcard of the mural we liked before she tells me she ought to be heading back. I try not to sound too disappointed, especially when she says, "I promise I'll stay longer next time. But my parents are gonna freak when they find me gone."

I can breathe a little easier. Apparently I haven't chased her off. We head back for the light-rail station and she buys her ticket, and while we're waiting I work up the nerve to say, "Thanks for coming. You know. I had fun." I scuff my shoe against the concrete.

She elbows me gently. Probably the first physical contact we've had all day. "You weren't kidding when you said you don't get out much."

"I don't get out ever." Not since moving. Not since Corey. There's been no one else. "Do you have friends you hang out with?"

Casper sighs and squints at nothing. "Once upon a time."

It's none of my business, but I'm curious. "What happened?"

"No one wants to be friends with a raving bitch." She purses her lips. "Which is what I became when I got sick. Chased off every last one of them, boyfriend included."

"You aren't a bitch to me."

"Because I realized after they were gone how shitty it was to be alone. It's horrible, you know? Not having anyone." She shrugs her thin shoulders and with that simple movement, I realize how small and frail she really is. "I used to be fat, too, did I tell you? But I had friends. Used to be fat and happy, now I'm skinny and miserable."

I try to remember a time when I was ever truly happy and can't. "I think I chased off my only friend, too."

"By being a raving bitch?"

"No." I hug myself. "By being me."

Casper starts to say something when the light-rail rumbles up ahead of us. She gives it a thoughtful look and, for a second, I'm desperately hoping she'll take a later train and stay. Just for awhile longer. So that I can tell her how Corey hates me now except when she feels sorry for me, and how everyone else I've ever known except for Maggie thought I was crazy.

But she sighs and punches my arm. "Then your friend wasn't really worth keeping around. Next time I come, you'll have to show me that bridge you were talking about."

I watch her multi-colored back and blonde hair retreat into the tram that carries her away.

SUICIDE WATCH

August

SUICIDE WATCH

CHAPTER 8

"You only have two weeks left, kiddo," Harold calls to remind me.

Where did the time go?

Maggie's house is nearly empty. The living room has been cleared save for the television, the little table it rests on, and a lamp. Her room is deserted. The halls, dining room, kitchen...all empty. If a stranger were to walk in, they'd have suspected I was some squatter hiding away in my room — the only one that remains unchanged.

Harold's right, I guess. It takes me no time at all to pack up my meager belongings, though it doesn't solve the question of where I'm supposed to go. I want to stay near here. I want to be close to the bridge. To Maggie.

I should have taken Harold up on his offer to help me look for a place. I check out three apartment complexes in the neighborhood, both of which are seedy, overpriced, and look like the carpets have been scrubbed with dirt. I may not be picky about my living arrangements, but I don't want roaches crawling across my face in the middle of the night. They creep me out.

I find another complex on the other side of the bridge, so it's farther than I'd like, but close enough. Closer to the light-rail station and the animal shelter, at least. The grounds are quiet when I pull up. In the leasing office is a curly-haired blonde girl in her late twenties, popping bubble-gum and typing noisily with her long nails. I linger near the door, shifting my weight from one foot to the other, and wait to be noticed.

Eventually she stops and looks up. "Oh, I'm sorry, sweetie. Are you here to drop off rent for your parents?"

A faint flush finds its way to my face. "I don't live here. I'm looking for a place."

SUICIDE WATCH

"Oh." Her eyes widen, but she stands and comes over to offer her hand. "I'm Laney. Sorry about that. You just look..." Laney pauses and smiles. "Nevermind. Anyway, come have a seat, mister—?"

I hate it when people call me that. "Vincent." I shake her hand and let her usher me into a chair.

"Vincent." She slides a brochure of floor-plans over to me. "What kind of apartment are you looking for, Vincent?"

"I don't know," I admit. Which is the answer I gave to every other place. Rather than try to shove a sales spiel down my throat, though, Laney gestures to the brochure and gives me a second to look it all over. I don't know how to tell whether or not I want to live in a place by tiny boxes with dimensions written inside.

"Do you have..." I pause, slide the brochure back to her, "anything...second floor. Overlooking the river?"

Laney clicks away at her computer and turns the monitor to show me a diagram of the complex I don't quite understand. "Well, we have a nice two-bedroom here. A townhouse down this way... And there's a little studio right in here, see? I'm not sure what the view is like." She glances at my face and when I say nothing, she offers, "I can take you to see it, if you want?"

We load into her golf cart after she's fetched a set of keys and rumble across the complex. I can almost smell the river from here. When we tromp up the concrete staircase to the top and she fumbles with the lock, she says, "Studio apartments aren't all too impressive, you know. Just one big room. So if you have anyone else living with you...?"

I step inside when Laney ushers me in. "No. Just me."

She's right about the place being small. Smaller than small. The main room might be the size of Maggie's dining and living room combined. There's a sliding glass door leading to a patio, a kitchen area in one corner, and a single door that leads—I assume—to a bathroom of equally tiny proportions.

But none of that really matters. It's only me. I don't know what I'd do with a lot of room anyway. All I care about is the view.

I pull open the sliding door and step onto the porch. There are some trees in the way, but once fall hits and the leaves thin out, I'll have a clear view of the Woodshire Bridge. Laney steps up beside me, hands on her hips. "Water and garbage is paid. Pets are allowed, with a small monthly fee. The community's pretty quiet, for the most part. Got a couple of college kids living next door that can get kinda loud on the weekends."

"I'll take it."

"Great." She smiles her sweet, cherry-lip-glossed smile at me. "Let's head back to the office and I'll have you fill out an application and run a credit check..."

Frowning, I turn to face her. "What if I don't have any credit?"

She nods, like she was worried about that. "No rental history, I'm guessing?" When I shake my head no, she hmm's. "Credit cards? Student loans? No?"

"Nothing, no." Before she can say anything, I add on helplessly, "I can pay for it all upfront. Can I do that? If I sign for six months, I can give you the whole amount of rent?"

Laney's eyes widen, but I know I've got her. Maybe I could've gotten away with paying a higher deposit or something, but if something happens to me in the next few months, I'd hate for Laney to be stuck trying to find new tenants on short-notice.

She claps me on the back. "All right, honey. Let's sign you up and get you a key."

By the weekend, I've gotten everything moved from

SUICIDE WATCH

Maggie's house to my new apartment. Everything fit into the van with a couple trips, though I had to struggle with my mattress and take apart the metal rolling frame. Getting it all up the stairs by myself was the biggest obstacle of it all.

I give Maggie's key over to Harold on my last trip, and we stand in the living room and look around. He double-checked all the closets and cabinets to make sure I hadn't forgotten anything. Now we're looking at the skeleton of my and Maggie's home, and I try to feel something other than resentment and abject fear of *what happens now?*

Harold takes a deep breath and pockets the key. "So... How do you like your new place?"

I shrug. Haven't stayed there yet; my bed was the first thing I took over this morning. "It's a place."

He nods. We head outside and lock the door. Every step of the way, I fight back the blistering panic, the thrum of my pulse and my heart in my throat, begging me to get back inside. This is home. Somehow, some way...things need to go back to how they were. I am not strong enough to do this.

But I stand there and watch Harold lock it all away, and I do nothing.

When he turns to me, I think he might be a little misty-eyed himself. "Vincent, look. I know this is all really... Just really shitty. Everything you've been through." He places his hands on my shoulders and leans down, leaving me with little choice but to look him in the eye. "It isn't fair. None of it is, and you sure don't deserve getting tossed out there on your own. I want you to keep my number and call me if there's *anything* I can do, anything I can help you with. All right?"

My stomach coils with embarrassment at his pity. I don't want anyone feeling sorry for me. But I assure him, "I'll keep your number." I tell myself I'll make sure to delete it if I die, so whoever finds me doesn't call him thinking he's family. So he never has to know what happened to me. He can go on with life thinking I moved on, grew up into some nice, upstanding, and well-balanced guy.

Harold offers to treat me to dinner, but I politely decline with an easy *maybe some other time*. I'm tired and sore, and I still have boxes to haul from the van to my apartment.

My apartment.

That sounds so weird.

With the table, bed, and television in place, the studio doesn't really look all that small. There's still plenty of floor space. I sold my computer desk, figuring I didn't *need* one when I had a laptop. The only other piece of furniture I own is a shelf with a meager helping of books and some video games. It looks more empty and lonely than it used to, but I don't know what to fill it with. I'm an avid music downloader and CDs are a waste of time. I'm not big on reading.

I set my laptop on the floor beside my bed and leave it on so I can listen to Paul McCartney and Wings sing me to sleep. Thinking about how to fill that emptiness in my life. That stupid empty shelf.

SUICIDE WATCH

September

SUICIDE WATCH

CHAPTER 9

Casper: I was beginning to think you'd ditched me.

I apologize again when I email back. *I didn't think about having to get internet hooked up.*

She asks what my new place is like. I tell her it's small and dark and I should probably buy another lamp. But I confess to RoxWell the bare walls make me feel lonely.

Posters? He suggests in his one-word answer. It's an idea. Better than the blank I drew. I get dressed and drive a couple blocks away to a music shop that specializes in mostly used stuff. It's where I've purchased ninety percent of my video games. I make a line for the posters, but after flipping through twenty of artists and half-naked girls, I give up and opt for wandering the rest of the store. There's a display for the new *Calamity Kitty* album. Corey must be ecstatic.

In the back near the curtained-off 'must be 18 to enter' area, I locate a few walls of vinyl records. I've never listened to vinyls. Now that I think about it, it sort of makes me feel like I'm missing out on something. I wonder how different it is, hearing a voice on a record as it was originally intended to be heard.

Habit has me thinking *I can't afford this* until I remind myself that, yes, I can. Technically. I have money. A pretty good chunk of it, in fact. So if I want to buy things, I can, and there's no one to tell me what a stupid idea it is.

I start at A and work my way to Z, plucking out every album of The Beatles — solo stuff included — that I can find. I grab up some Queen, Bob Dylan, The Doors, Led Zeppelin, and Janis Joplin as I go, and take my armful of prizes to the front of the store where the clerk gives me a funny but amused look. Of course I don't have a record player, but the shop has portable turntables and I snatch one of those, too.

"Light shopper. Sure there's nothing else you need?" the guy asks, looking over my selection. My face reddens and I mutter *no* under my breath. He rings me up, I pay, then go home to struggle with my things up the stairs because making more than one trip doesn't cross my mind.

The vinyls don't take up anywhere near all the space on my shelf, but it fills a portion and makes the whole apartment look better. A real person lives here. I get the turntable unwrapped, plugged in and spinning, so I can pull out a record — *Revolver* — and figure out how to start it up. There's a faint crackle before George Harrison's voice hums through with *Taxman*. I stretch out on the floor in the near darkness next to the turntable, and close my eyes.

I listen until track one turns to track two, and I like the way it sounds. Deeper, heavier than a CD or mp3. I can't explain it. Then John Lennon comes on and my eyes open. *I'm Only Sleeping.* One of my favorites.

I get it. More than any other song he wrote.
This.

This is why people listen to records, I decide. Because the sound of his voice, so low and melancholy, breaks my heart in a hundred different ways it never has before. It's hard to breathe. Because every word of the song is true, and I know he wrote it in a period of his life where he, too, was at a loss. Drowning in apathy and sleeping away his days. People said he was lazy, that fame had gotten to him. They were too blind to realize laziness had nothing to do with it. He was *sad*. Sad, and on the verge of an internal meltdown that would overturn his life and everything he'd worked so hard for.

I wonder if that's me. If I'm on the edge of some big crisis that'll send me spinning out of orbit and into living some bizarre existence where everyone I encounter will

think I'm completely nuts.
    I'd sooner throw myself off a bridge before that happens.

SUICIDE WATCH

CHAPTER 10

From: HARBINGER <admin@yoursuicidewatch.com>

To: NowhereMan <herecomesthesun@beemail.com>

Subject: SW Activity

hello new SW member! i'm sure you've seen me around, but i'm harbinger, the site admin. I noticed your posting level was pretty low and you have not been very active on the forums. we generally make it a rule to only keep active accounts open for security reasons.

no worries. i'm only wondering if you're having problems settling in, and if there's anything i can do to help.

sometimes verbalizing our pain, and discussing out plans for end-of-life happenings is difficult. i like all my website members to feel comfortable talking with me about these things. have you put thought into your end-of-life plans?

best regards,

harbinger (site admin)

SUICIDE WATCH

CHAPTER 11

I have a message from Casper that night asking if I'm busy tomorrow, and if I want to hang out. *We could see the bridge,* she tells me.

I'm almost possessive over the bridge. Like what I witnessed there is a secret no one else is privy to. But I've already told her and I guess if anyone's going to share it with me, it ought to be one of the only sort-of friends I have.

After I email her back with a time, she responds: *Any objections to me bringing RoxWell along? He wants to meet you.* I freeze, fingers hovering over the keys.

She wants to bring...

I get that they're friends. But it never occurred to me they hung out in person. Or had ever met face-to-face. I have a mental image of RoxWell approaching me out of nowhere, reciting a few lines from a song, and running away. The thought of meeting him—and that *he* wants to meet *me*—makes me feel nauseous.

Yeah. That's cool.

The next day at the light-rail station, I have no idea what to expect. I don't know a thing about this guy. *He's shy,* Casper said. Not exactly a lot to go by. What else did she say? That he has a bad home life.

RoxWell has parents who don't care.

Casper has parents who care too much.

NowhereMan has no parents at all.

Casper's stark blonde hair is the first thing I see. She's leaning against a brick wall and her mouth is moving. If it's possible, her face is thinner and more tired than it was when I saw her last. She has on the same sort of obnoxious brightly colored clothes.

The guy standing next to her can only be RoxWell. I can't see much of him. He's got on jeans, and his black jacket is all zipped up even though it won't really get cold until October. A striped black and white scarf hangs around his neck and he's got on this Greek fisherman's style hat — and the only reason I know what kind of hat it is, is because John Lennon wore the same kind. With the way he's got his head down, I can't see anything of his face other than a mop of dark hair falling into it.

Casper spots me and straightens up, not waving because she sees me heading their way. We don't do the whole huggy-clingy thing me and Corey used to do. I'm worried I would break her. "Hey," I greet instead.

"Hey yourself." She peers up at me. The prominent dark circles under her eyes make them look an even brighter shade of blue. "We're starving. Any place to eat around here before we catch a movie?"

I shrug, casting a glance at RoxWell, who still has his head down, studying his feet. "Yeah, sure. Burgers? There's a place across the street from the theater."

"Sounds good." She nudges her companion with an elbow. "So, Vincent, this is Adam Rockswell. Adam, this is Vincent Hazelwood."

Rockswell. RoxWell. Oh. Original. "Nice to meet you." I always feel stupid offering out a hand to people my age, and yet I'm doing just that. Adam — can I call him Adam? — stares at it for so long that I think I might stand here forever, until he slowly lifts his own hand to shake mine. His fingers are cold. But he looks up a little, and under that hair he's got a thin mouth and these big, gold eyes that have me staring like an idiot and wanting to ask if he wears contacts for that kind of color. I think it must be the way the sun's reflecting off his face to make them that bright.

"Yeah," he says, casual, in a voice that's a lot softer than I expected. "Hey."

Casper's already prodding her fingers into my ribs and I take the hint, leading them both to Maggie's ugly van. "Traveling in *style*, boys," she says as she hops into the front seat. I blush, thinking maybe I ought to trade in the van for something less humiliating.

I take them to Zeke's Burgers across from the theaters in town. It's the sort of place where you order at the counter and they'll bring it to you when it's ready; a mix of fast-food meets traditional dining, I guess. As we're figuring out what to order, the cashier asks if this is all together. I answer "Yeah, I'm paying," before the others can speak up, because even if my ride is less than impressive I can at least be cool by buying them lunch.

Unfortunately, when we get our food Casper takes two bites of her burger, nibbles on a fry, and pushes the basket away. Her head lolls back and she sighs. I pause in mid-bite.

"Is it okay? Is there something wrong with it?"

"No, it's fine."

I start to ask why she isn't eating when I remember what she mentioned in one of her various emails. Something about food. And eating. And how she lost a bunch of weight because the treatments made her nauseous all the time. Maybe I should've taken her somewhere else, with food that would've been easier on her stomach. Her third round of treatments started last week. I wonder if her hair will fall out again.

Adam, though, is scarfing down his burger like he's never tasted anything better. At least someone's enjoying it. I don't know where he fits all that food into his thin little body.

"Did you know," Casper says after a few minutes filled with my and Adam's chewing and occasional straw-slurping, "Rox is a musician? He plays guitar and sings."

My spine straightens to attention. Obviously, I did know that because she told me, but I get the impression I'm supposed to pretend this is the first I've heard of it. "Really?"

Adam lifts his head, chewing paused, mouth still full of food, looking like a deer caught in the headlights. He swallows quickly. "Why would you bring that up?"

Casper rolls her eyes. "Because you're sitting there with your head down and your mouth full like you'd rather be anywhere else and it's obnoxious. *Say something*."

His shoulders hunch up a little and he shrinks in on himself. He needs some coaxing, maybe. He hasn't spoken much to me, but I haven't really made an effort, either. I keep staring at his pretty eyes.

"So, uh, what kind of music do you play?"

He shrugs, taking another bite of his burger. Chewing. Giving himself time to work up to an answer. "Covers."

"Covers?"

"Other peoples' stuff. That's all."

Casper smacks her palm against the table. "Don't listen to him. He's really good. And he'd probably be awesome at writing his own stuff; he's just too scared to try."

Adam slouches, frowning at his fries.

I worry at my lower lip. Casper attempts another go at her burger, but two bites in she groans. "Bad idea." She crawls over me to get out of the booth and heads for the bathroom. I sigh.

"Don't feel sorry for her," Adam mutters around his straw.

"Why's that?"

"She knows what makes her sick. She knows she's in no shape to be out."

"Oh." Pause. "So why's she here?"

He shrugs. "Stubbornness."

I just want to be normal again, she'd told me.

Whether Adam thinks I should or not, when Casper returns with a pale face and an empty stomach, I do feel sorry for her.

"To hell with a movie," she says. "Let's go see that bridge."

☆

The Woodshire Bridge sits away from any busy streets, and it's kind of a rickety old thing I could swear you can feel swaying a little when you drive across. I take them the full length of the bridge and find a place to park within walking distance, so we can backtrack, following the trail I usually take when jogging. I've seen pictures of the Golden Gate bridge, and the suicide signs posted there with crisis numbers to dissuade jumpers. There's nothing like that here. And it's so abandoned the chances of being caught are slim.

Right at the spot where I watched Jessica jump, we stop. There's no fog this time so I can see straight down into the water churning below.

"This is it, huh." Casper braces her hands on the railing and leans over. "Oh my God, how could anyone seriously..."

Adam, I realize, is keeping behind me, eyes on the ground. A gust of wind makes the old bridge creek and groan a little, and by the way he seems to wince...

"Are you afraid of heights, Adam? We can go back."

He shrugs, doesn't look at me. His cheeks are a bit flushed. There's something about it, about his lack of an answer that hurts my feelings. I don't think he's made eye contact with me once since I picked them up from the station.

I turn away, arms crossed. "You really don't talk at all, do you?" I say. "If you don't like me, you didn't have to come, you know."

Adam's head snaps up, startled. "I didn't..."

"Didn't what? It's true. You talk to Casper." I glance at her and she nods. "But all I get are song lyrics and shrugs."

He shrugs, realizes he's just proved me right, and frowns. He's still not saying anything, and Casper begins to hum the theme to Jeopardy. Adam's mouth draws tight and thoughtful. "Why don't you have parents?"

I blink slowly and turn around to face him. "What?"

"You had a foster mom. What happened to your real parents?"

It's the first time he's met my eyes and not immediately looked away. "I...don't know."

"Were they Jewish, too? You look kind of Jewish."

Casper punches him in the arm. He doesn't seem to feel it. "That was offensive on so many levels. You can't just tell someone they look like a Jew."

"Judaism isn't even a race," I mutter.

Adam's cheeks redden, but I can tell by the way he looks at me so helplessly he doesn't understand what he did wrong. He was just trying to talk, to ask questions, because I told him he should, because he...doesn't want me to think he hates me? I don't know. But he was trying and that's all that matters to me.

"I don't know what happened with my mom and dad." I frown at nothing in particular. "I was really little, so maybe they died."

"Like in a car accident?"

"Maybe."

The truth is, I *do* know what happened to my parents. They were young and they realized a baby wasn't what they wanted or needed, so they gave me up. I've never understood how a mom and dad can have a kid for two and a half years before deciding, *no, nevermind, just kidding. Can we take it back?*

I suspect they exchanged me for a cat. Cheaper. Less work.

Adam opens his mouth to say something further, but he halts, eyes going wide. I turn to see what he's staring at behind me, and we watch as Casper hauls herself over the railing of the bridge.

My heart stops. Frozen. I can't make myself move to grab her.

Casper doesn't jump. She positions herself carefully on the outer lip of the bridge in the same spot Jessica did, arms behind her, hanging onto the rail, but not as tightly as I think she ought to.

"Casper—"

She looks back at us with a grin. "What? Oh, come on; don't look at me like that. I'm not gonna jump. You should try this, though. The view..." Her face turns away from us. The wind whips and pulls at her short hair and bright clothes, wanting to pluck her off the bridge and into the river below. I imagine her tiny body hitting the surface, bones shattering into a million pieces before the water even enters her lungs. Instant death.

Then I think of her dying as she is now. The sickness eating away at her insides until there's nothing left. Which one would really be harder to watch?

I don't let myself think as I move forward and swing a leg over the rail to join her. Adam's breath hitches, but he doesn't follow.

The ledge isn't even wide enough for my feet to fit on completely. I hang onto the rail tightly and do as Casper does...leaning out slowly over the water. Like this, there is no safety. No rail to catch me if I slip. I'm almost flying. Between me and death, there is...nothing. Nothing in the way but my own decision to hang on.

For a second, that thought, that feeling...is freeing.

"You feel like you could float away," Casper whispers. I think it's something I'm not meant to hear.

"Guys..."

Adam's voice is so soft, so pleading and lonely and it drags me back. Away from the water, back over the railing alongside Casper until our feet are planted firmly on the ground again. He's watching us with eyes so wide I can see myself in them. His shoulders are squared tightly with tension.

I am guilty.

I bite my lip. Casper must notice it, too, because she groans and puts her arms around Adam's neck. "Hey, don't look like that. We weren't gonna jump."

"I know that," he mutters. But with the way he doesn't meet our eyes, I'm not so sure he does.

☆

I don't want to bring Adam and Casper home with me because it isn't much of a home to show off. But Casper insists and I'm out of ideas for where else we should go. So I drive back to the apartment complex and lead them into my gloomy abode next to the noisy neighbors, where the single lamp illuminates only a small corner of the studio.

Shrugging out of my coat, I make it a point not to look at my guests. "I would give you the tour, but, uh, here it is."

Casper ventures inside without hesitation, shimmying out of her jacket and tossing it onto my bed. "This is awesome."

"Not really, no."

"Yeah, it is. It's your own place. How cool is that? I'd kill for a place of my own." When she puts it that way...I guess it is kind of cool. She stands in the center of the room. It looks bigger with her there because she's so small. The walls might swallow her up.

Adam doesn't take off his coat, but he looks around. The second his eyes lock onto my records leaning against the turntable, he's drawn to them like there are magnets in his fingertips. He crouches, but doesn't touch. Casper throws herself onto my bed and stretches out. I take a seat beside her.

"You can look at them, if you want," I say to Adam. "They don't bite."

He glances at me and carefully begins rifling through the records.

"You know what you need?" Casper says, rolling onto her side to face me. "A dog. You should totally get a dog."

That suggestion catches me off-guard. I look at her. *Really* look at her. I haven't told either of them about my frequent animal shelter trips. "I'm not going to adopt something that'll get attached to me just so I can leave it all alone."

An indescribable veil slides down over her expression and her mouth draws thin.

"That's sort of what your foster mom did to you, isn't it?" Adam says.

Casper's mouth drops open, but she can't even find the words to chastise him. Adam looks between her and me, seems to realize he's said something wrong and turns away quickly. I bite my lip, chewing at the skin there.

It's true, isn't it? I'm the dog Maggie brought home. The stray that needed a home. And she left me all alone. It wasn't her fault. How many times did she tell me I was going to give her a heart-attack one of these days?

I swallow back the lump in my throat. "Do you guys want pizza for dinner?"

There's an enthusiastic *yes* which comes primarily from Casper, and I get up to place an order online. Maggie used to be obsessive about using coupons. It was the only time she'd order pizza, when the coupons came in the mail. And she always had to call it in. Never any of that 'fancy computer techno stuff you kids do.'

Adam pulls out one of my records, *Sheer Heart Attack*, and puts it on to play. Casper listens to a verse or two while I clack away on my laptop, before she says, "This is pretty good. Who is it?"

Adam slowly turns around to give her an incredulous, narrow-eyed stare. "How can you not recognize Freddie Mercury's voice?" he asks. Her expression is blank.

I pause in my typing. "Freddie Mercury. Queen?"

"Oh... Yeah, I've heard of him."

"*Them*. They're a band. You've heard their music, right?"

Shrug. "The stuff that plays on the radio."

Adam and I exchange unimpressed looks. Freddie sings how it's funny but there's nothing to laugh about. I order a large pizza, a few sodas, and some cheese-sticks.

Online. Without a coupon.

CHAPTER 12

After we stuff ourselves on dinner, Casper falls asleep on my bed. There's nowhere in the apartment for me and Adam to talk without waking her, so we drag a few blankets onto the balcony and stare at the river.

I kept putting thought into telling them about the email from Harbinger, but I didn't know how to broach the subject. *Hey, the leader of the site is getting impatient that I haven't socialized more or offed myself. What should I do?*

Besides, if I told them about his email, I would have to tell them I wrote back and told him, vaguely, I did have a plan, I just wasn't sure whether or not I wanted to use it yet.

Adam interrupts my thoughts by asking, "Don't you get lonely here?"

I glance at him like I'm not sure if he's actually initiating conversation with me or I'm imagining it. "Sometimes. A little. I mean, I have neighbors all around, so it's not like I'm alone."

"You're just telling yourself that to feel better."

"I guess so." I poke my toes out from beneath my blanket, pressing them to the worn metal of the balcony railings, while being completely unsure what to make of his observation. "At least I have a place. Aren't I supposed to be grateful for that? I could be homeless. Stuck on the streets." If it weren't for Maggie's money, I would be.

"I don't buy it." Adam's brows draw tightly together. He has his blanket cocooned all around him, even hooded about his head. "People are always saying things like that."

"Things like what?"

"*Other people have it worse, so you should be grateful for what you have.* Like that. It's not fair."

"But it's true. Things could always be worse. We could be digging our dinner out of the dumpsters behind

SUICIDE WATCH

Safeway and hope the expiration dates don't really mean anything. But instead, we're here." My gaze drifts back out over the water. From here it is a black and eerie sight. "With full stomachs, central heat and air, warm showers and—"

"And sometimes none of that matters." He hunches forward in such a way his hair and blanket obscure his face and I can't see him. "It doesn't matter if it could be worse, because even those people living on the street could still say 'it's not as bad as it could be.' You still feel the pain. It still matters. All this means nothing unless you have people around who understand you. People who get that, sometimes, you're just...really, really fucking sad and it's for no reason at all. Then you get pissed off 'cause you realize you're upset without a good reason, and you feel even worse."

I open my mouth, but no words come out.

Because he's right. I *am* sad. I'm sad a lot, for no reason at all. I've lost Maggie, sure, but even before then, I alternated from being completely indifferent to everything, and feeling so, so sad all the time, and it drove her crazy. It drove Corey crazy, too. Maybe that's why she doesn't want to be my friend anymore.

A sting of tears catches me off-guard. I haven't cried lately. Not over Maggie, not over losing the house or...anything. Except applesauce. I curl in on myself and pull the blanket over my head. If I can't see Adam, I don't want him to see me, either. I don't want him to see that I'm crying over being sad about *being sad* and not over the things that should really matter.

A few minutes pass before I feel Adam shifting closer. His side presses against mine. "I'm sorry," he mumbles. "I didn't mean to upset you."

"You didn't upset me. *I* upset me." Thinking I ought to move away from him and actually doing it are two different things. I stay right where I'm at. I can sort of feel the warmth of him through our blankets.

"The last time I cried was when Maggie died. Over applesauce."

"Applesauce?"

"I couldn't get the jar open. It was just...a jar. A stupid jar. I couldn't get it open, and I burst into tears. I can't even cry for real reasons that real people cry over. Like someone dying." The dam has been broken. The tears are coming freely now, soaking the bit of blanket I'm pressing my face into. This is the sort of thing I fought so hard to hide from Maggie and Corey, but it was inevitable. You can't hide this sort of crazy from someone close to you.

But Adam doesn't tell me I'm being unreasonable or stupid or crazy. He pushes his blanket-hood back and tips his face, trying to peer at me. For awhile, he only watches the tears sliding down my cheeks like he's trying to figure them out.

"You know, I ruined the carpet of our dining room once."

I can't help but tilt my head just enough to watch him with one blurry eye.

"What...?"

"My parents were having a dinner party after we moved into our new house. I'd had a really bad day." He pulls his legs up and props his chin atop his knees. "Dad told me I had to stay in my room and not talk to anybody. He always thought...I don't know. I guess he didn't want me meeting his coworkers because he was embarrassed of me. They wanted to show off the house, not their son.

"And I was just...so mad and my feelings were hurt. Mom told me I was being too sensitive. She's always telling me that." A tiny, embarrassed smile pulls at his lips. "So I made myself a sandwich, and threw the jar of jelly on the brand new white carpet. Shattered. Made a huge mess. Left this ugly purple stain. Mom about had a nervous breakdown."

I sniff quietly. "You did it on purpose?"

"Yeah. I felt really bad for it later, but at the time I think I just wanted to be noticed. It didn't work, other than..." He trails off quickly, and I think I see him rubbing his arm as he looks away, like he's remembering an old war wound. "I did all this stuff wanting them to pay attention to me. Then my dad passed away, and Mom...she wouldn't even notice if I pierced every inch of my body and grew a mohawk except to tell me I was humiliating her."

"So you stopped trying."

He ducks his head, running his fingers through the dark hair along the nape of his neck. "Yeah. I guess I did."

I want to reach out to touch that hair. Slide my fingers through it. It's unkempt, but looks so soft. I want to curl up against him, around him, and tell him I understand. I don't have a family, and he's invisible to his. I want to tell him that *I* notice him, even if no one else does.

His shoulders hunch up, fingers lacing behind his neck. I know what he would say to that. *I'm not worth noticing.* And I'm not sure I can stomach him taking something so heartfelt and sincere and tossing it aside, so I say nothing. We sit on the balcony, hip to hip, being sad together.

CHAPTER 13

Harold calls four days later and asks if I want to have lunch. I pull back and stare at the phone like he's lost his mind, which I think he must have. Inwardly, a small part of me panics. Did something happen? Was I not really supposed to get that money?

"Relax, kiddo. I just wanted to see how you were doing."

I don't relax, but I agree to meet him at a diner in town tomorrow for lunch, not far from his office.

Harold looks as put-together as he always does in his suit and tie, with his graying hair slicked back. He's out of place in a diner like this, but I fit right in with my messy hair and a hole in the knee of my jeans. If he notices he doesn't belong here, he doesn't show it. He smiles while sliding into the other side of the booth.

"How's it going, Vince?"

I had already ordered my drink before he showed up, so I toy with the wrapper from the straw, glancing up only briefly. He makes me nervous. Why does he make me nervous? Maybe because he's been the bearer of bad news before, and I worry he'll do it again. "Fine, I guess." I can't think of a nice way to say *what do you want?*

"That's good." He folds his hands on the table. Didn't he used to wear a wedding ring? "I know this probably seemed out of left field, me asking you here. I just wanted to check up on you. See for myself you were doing all right."

I nod. Probably a little too fast and purposefully to be believable. "Yeah. No. That's cool. I'm fine, obviously, as you can see. I'm not dead or anything." Yet.

"What have you been up to?"

Oh. Joining pro-suicide forums, meeting strangers online, contemplating the meaning of life.

For one brief second, I'm terrified Harold knows

precisely what I've been up to. He has a briefcase of notes on me; my internet search history, my comings and goings, the number of times in a week I jog out to the bridge and consider throwing myself off.

    God, please tell me I don't look as panicked as I feel.
"Sorry?"

"Well," Harold gestures at nothing in particular. A waitress comes over long enough to ask *coffee?* to which Harold gives her a smile and a nod before looking at me again. "Are you working? Thinking about going to college? Maggie talked about that. About college."

"Oh." Relax, self. "I don't...know. I haven't really..." The words trail off, lost in the air all around us, because it isn't his business and I wouldn't know how to explain it. What would he say if he knew I spend most of my days in bed, wanting to sleep and unable to make myself move? I do nothing. Absolutely nothing. Because it's all so much effort.

Harold takes a deep breath. "Vincent. You're legally an adult now. I almost wish you weren't, because I would've taken you in and been able to keep a better eye on you otherwise."

I give him a funny look, but say nothing.

"You haven't had it easy. You've had it pretty shitty, frankly. The day you came home with Maggie, she called me up and told me she wanted to go over her will, so she could leave what little she had to you."

"I don't want to talk about this," I mumble around my straw.

"Something drew Maggie to you. She could be hard to deal with at times, but, God, she loved you to pieces. And if anything ever happened..."

"What's it matter to you?" I do not want to talk about this and it makes my heart hurt because I don't want to be guilted into anything because it's what *Maggie would have wanted*. She's dead so what the hell is the point?

Harold doesn't look the least bit phased. "Why

wouldn't it matter to me?"

"Because you were her lawyer, and she's dead now," I snap. "She's dead, and you can't work for dead people. You can't say goodbye to them, you can't make them proud, you can't live for them. So, again, what's it matter to you? You don't know me."

I start to get up. Harold doesn't try to stop me. Not with physical force, anyway, though what he says stops me in my tracks: "Maggie's son, Allen, was my best friend growing up."

Maggie had a kid. That much I knew. He died overseas ages ago, probably before I was born. I don't even know which war. I've never given him much thought because Maggie never wanted to talk about him when I asked.

"Maggie liked to pretend she was all right." Harold laces his fingers together, studying the spot where I was sitting a moment ago. "She was strong like that. But Allen always told me to keep an eye on his mom when he wasn't around because she got lonely a lot. Didn't do too well on her own. So after he died, I tried to check up on her, you know? Me and my wife both. Just to let her know someone was still around who cared. She had already lost her husband and now she'd lost her kid. She didn't have anyone else." Finally, Harold tilts his head, meeting my eyes before I have the chance to look away. "She told me years later that my family was the only reason she didn't kill herself. Then she brought you home, and she told me that you remind her a lot of herself during that time."

I am suffocated with this knowledge.

I try to picture Maggie giving up like that, just lying down and dying. Because she *was* so strong, so stubborn. I never saw her cry. Never saw her upset. She was stone while I fell apart over everything.

"My point to all this, Vince, is that you were the first thing in a very, very long time to come into Maggie's life that gave her purpose again." The sincerity in his eyes is too much. "If you're not okay, then let me help."

Yes. Yes, I want help. I want to not...feel like this anymore. Except then I wonder what it's like to feel *normal* because if you take away the things I've felt all my life — the insecurity, the pain, the loneliness, the absolute dissolution of any sane or rational thought during one of my more manic moods and the helplessness when I realize one of said manic moods is creeping up on me (like right now) — what's left after the fact? Emptiness?

I take medication that makes me feel absolutely nothing. Medication that scoops out my insides and leaves me hollow. Sometimes I take it because that emptiness is the only way to keep my heart from crumbling to pieces. This is what it is like inside my head, Harold; all these emotions and I do not know how to get them out.

So I smile without meaning it and I say, "No, really, you're overreacting. I'm totally okay."

And I apologize, but I'm not hungry and I have plans and I can't breathe, so I need to go, and I leave him there alone with his coffee.

CHAPTER 14

Good things happen to bad people, and bad things happen to good people. I don't consider myself one or the other, so I can't help but wonder if that's why I'm like this. Why I can feel so little in one second and so much in the next. Why it gets difficult to breathe and my chest hurts and my brain is full to bursting.

I rush home and barricade myself inside, huddling on my bed, and every breath is a conscious effort. In and out, in and out. If I weren't getting enough air, I would've passed out by now, right?

I want to call Casper. Or Adam. I want to hear the voice of someone who might reassure me it's okay and I am not crazy and it will pass. Casper would probably tell me to stop being overdramatic. Adam might sit right beside me and say nothing at all, but his nearness would help. It would be enough.

Corey would freak out and not have a clue what to do with me. Like she did last time.

To be fair, I sort of misled her into thinking I was normal. I guess. Any freak-outs I had, I never let her see. Any thoughts one might not consider exactly 'normal,' I bit back. You know: if you can't say something sane, don't say anything at all.

Then I found out I was moving. My foster home wanted me out, Maggie wanted me to move in with her, and it meant I was being taken away from Corey. When I got upset over this fact, she tried to say, "It's okay, Vinny," and for some reason...it set me off. I accused her of not caring. I threw glasses on the floor and stepped on the broken pieces in my bare feet. I cried and I hyperventilated and ranted that, no, it wasn't fucking *okay*, it was never going to *be* okay, and I was so exhausted from people shoving me aside and getting rid of me when it suited and why should I have to move when Maggie would get tired of me in a few months, anyway?

It was why I refused any time she brought up wanting to officially adopt me. It would be one more problem for the day she kicked me out. But Maggie never got rid of me. Still, even up until the day she died, I think a part of me was still waiting for it.

What do I have to show for it? A high school diploma I never cared about in the first place. A lonely apartment. And there's me, sitting here in the dark, convincing myself I'm not dying, not sure if I would care if I were, and too afraid to call the people I think are my friends because I'd likely chase them off like I have with everyone else who has ever mattered.

When I've calmed down enough to move again, I put on one of my Beatles records and let *Hey Jude* fill the air. Once there are voices other than the sound of my own in my head, I can lie down on the middle of the floor, close my eyes, and focus on the music instead of everything else.

I stay there for the duration of the record. Breathing in, breathing out. Long after it's silent again and I'm only vaguely aware I'm falling asleep. Or too exhausted to move, anyway. When I wake up, it's near nine P.M. Meaning, I've slept my afternoon and evening away and I'm going to be up all night.

Guess it's a good thing Casper is online all hours of the day and night. Me, her, and Adam buckled down and installed an instant messenger program so as soon as I'm online, she IMs me.

Casper: Isn't it past your bedtime, young man?

Me: Just woke up. What a lovely sunset.

Casper: You okay? Rox said he called you earlier and you didn't answer.

Oh. Where is my phone? Why did he call? What would he have said? Adam is so quiet in person, I can't even imagine what he'd be like on the phone. I'd spend forever sitting there, listening to him breathe.

You know, that doesn't sound so bad.

Me: Long day. Nothing major. How are you feeling?

Casper: Same ol', same ol'. The Parents are reluctantly going out of town this weekend. Cousin's wedding. I convinced them not to worry about me and go have a good time.

Me: And they aren't making you go?

Casper: Long car rides make me queasy. They don't make me do much that I don't want to do anymore. Which means we should totally do something while they're gone.

Me: Like what?

Casper: Sleepover. Rent some bad movies. I haven't been out of my house overnight in like a year.

Sleepover.

I've had Casper and Adam over several times now, but never overnight. We wander downtown or hang out here for a few hours before I have to take them back to the light-rail station. I haven't had a *sleepover* in...actually, I've never had one, come to think of it. There were a few nights I crashed at Corey's place, but I always got woken up by her parents and shuffled off before it could be considered a 'sleepover.' I guess I have the room. And I don't really know how to tell Casper no.

So I tell her sure, great idea, I'll buy the snacks. Which is sort of a given anymore, because Casper can't exactly ask her folks for money when she's supposed to be at home resting, and Adam's mom hardly remembers he exists.

Friday evening, I pick them up from the light-rail station. Despite her grinning, Casper looks incredibly drained. And it's only going to get worse, I realize, because whatever treatment they've been trying obviously isn't working. I don't comment on it, though. Even I'm not so socially inept as to greet her with *you look like shit*.

We pile into the van and head back to my place with a detour to the store to pick up sodas and snacks. When we march up the steps and into my apartment, it's with potato chips, ice-cream, pizza rolls, Oreos, and soda. I'm going to wake up three hundred pounds heavier in the morning.

I order us a pizza again because I don't have much in the way of actual food and Adam, according to Casper, loves the place we ordered from last time. I can't help but be envious she gets all these little details out of him when he hardly speaks to me, but then I remember how we sat on the balcony and told each other how sad we are, and I think it's a fair trade.

We get through half a movie before dinner arrives. Then we sit in a circle on the middle of the floor, eating, and Casper says, "Can you put on some more of that Queen music?"

Adam and I exchange looks. I shrug. He shoves a pepperoni into his mouth and scoots over to the turntable to put on *Night at the Opera*. Casper bobs her head a little. She's picking at her food more than eating it. I think something is on her mind.

"You didn't even know who Freddie Mercury was, and now you're requesting his music?" I ask.

She shrugs. "I went home and listened to some things online. I like it."

"There might be hope for you yet."

"Hey, there is nothing wrong with my music tastes." She abandons her pizza slice and wipes her greasy fingertips on a napkin. "I read up on him some, too. Like how he died and all that."

Another look shared between me and Adam and I wonder if he's thinking what I'm thinking: where is this leading? I hope Casper didn't call this little get-together in order to talk about dying. Which is a stupid thought considering death is what brought us into each others' lives to begin with.

"Anyway." Casper waves her napkin like a white flag. "I wanted to talk to you guys, since we're here."

Adam licks a spot of sauce from his bottom lip. It makes me want to keep staring at his mouth. "About...?"

"Joey's dead."

My head snaps up. Adam quickly swallows his bite of pizza. "What? I thought he was still—"

"Trying treatment. Yeah. He was." Casper picks at her pepperoni. "According to the last few emails he sent, anyway. He shot himself."

Adam and I say nothing, too stunned to know what *to* say. Casper never met Joey. In fact, she's only mentioned him to me a handful of times. But he was, to her, a kindred spirit of sorts. Someone dealing with the same everyday pain and torment she herself was going through. But last I heard, Joey was keeping his chin up, not ready to throw in the towel. Not just yet.

What the hell happened?

Casper has her head down. "I convinced my parents to let me stop treatment."

Double-whammy.

We go still.

This shouldn't surprise me like it does. The first conversation Casper and I ever had, she said she was sick of chemo and radiation and would rather enjoy what time she had left without it. But knowing someone wants to change something and actually having them change it is different.

Adam opens his mouth, closes it again. Words are lost to him. So it's up to me to ask, "What does that mean?"

"It means I've got three months, at the outset, if I'm lucky." She props her elbows on her knees and refuses to look at either of us. "Maybe less, but no more. And who knows how much of that time I'll be...functional."

I try to imagine someone as bright and noisy as Casper bed-ridden and I don't like it. She's always so full of energy. Even when she's tired and hurting, you can see in her eyes it's only skin-deep. Mentally, she's so restless she can't stand it. The world moves around Casper in blinding blurs of color and she wants nothing more than to be a part of it, except now her body won't let her keep up.

Functional. Like she's some kind of machine.

"You're getting to a point," I say. A point that has nothing to do with stopping treatment or having a few months left to live.

"Yeah." Casper pushes her thin shoulders back, straightens, finally looks up to meet our inquiring stares. "I want to know if, when it's time, when I'm *done*, if I can count on you for help." Before I can open my mouth, she adds, "I don't mean I want you to shoot me in the face or something. I mean, if I call you up one night and ask you to come get me, will you?"

In that moment, I ought to be feeling a thousand things. Horror. Fear. Sadness. I reach for it and all I can find is the numb sort of weariness I felt when I watched Jessica jump off the bridge. Because that's what Casper wants. When she's ready, she wants us to take her to the Woodshire Bridge.

She wants us to take her to die.

"That's not fair," Adam murmurs in a wobbly voice. "You're asking us to help—you want us to...watch you die?"

Casper's expression doesn't change. "I'm asking you to help me go the way I want to go. I'm asking you to help, if I can't do it myself, because the last thing I want is to spend my last days like a lump in a bed, unable to do anything, needing help to eat or shower or take a shit. I want to go out with some dignity."

Adam's jaw clenches. "When your parents go down to the morgue to identify your body, what's going to be dignified about that?"

Half a second is the calm before the storm. Half a second, and I'm leaning back, away from them, because Casper explodes and lurches to her feet, knocking over her soda, arms spread wide.

"You have no right to be judgmental!" she shrieks. "You. Have. No. *Right*. How did we even meet, Adam? We all met because we're *sick* of living, because you two wanted to give it all up, just like I do!"

My hands are over my ears. I hate shouting, I hate it I hate it I hate it. Adam sets his jaw, stares up at Casper unflinching, but I can see the slight tremble to his mouth. He doesn't like it, either. "Is this because of Joey? He dies and you decide you're done?"

"Oh, *fuck you*. It has nothing to do with him."

"Then how can you just...plan it out so calmly? Put an expiration date on your *existence?*"

"Because unlike you two," she hisses, scooping up her soda, "I. Am. *Unfixable*."

The mostly empty can hits the wall with a metallic clink that sounds as hollow as I feel.

We are all broken. Every one of us.

Casper cannot be fixed.

For the first time, the gravity of what that really means hits me. There is no changing her mind because dying is not up to her. She is going to die. Even if we don't take her to the bridge and watch her jump, we'll still be witnessing her death...it will just be a slower process.

"I'll do it." The silence is almost louder than the sound of my voice. "If that's really what you want...then I'll do it."

They look at me as though they've only just remembered I'm here. Adam's expression scrunches up into a multitude of things — uncertainty, sadness, anger, loss — before settling on resignation. "...Yeah. Me, too."

Just like that, the storm is over. Her energy spent, Casper's shoulders slump, the angry fire in her eyes extinguished.

She says, whisper-soft, "Thank you," and picks her soda can off my floor.

CHAPTER 15

We stay up all hours of the night, alternating between watching movies, eating too much, and listening to records while talking about nothing at all.

Or rather, Adam and Casper talk. Mainly Casper. They have stories. Funny ones, about school and life. Adam's stories are funny only in retrospect—like the time in Freshman year he got chased halfway home by two Juniors who accused him of watching them in the showers after gym—and probably weren't funny at all at the time, but rather utterly terrifying and humiliating.

I don't have much to add. Any stories I can call to mind have to do with Corey or Maggie or hurting myself or breaking things, all of which I don't feel much like bringing up. Talking about people you miss, people you've lost, things you've done, is like ripping open an old wound. Doesn't hurt any less than it did the first time. If I don't think about them, don't talk about them, I can stop hurting over it. Focus on the people who are *here* right this minute.

Casper and Adam are my beautiful distractions.

We sleep until lunch, munch on cold pizza and watch another movie, so by the time we pack up and leave, it's creeping into evening again. When we get to the light-rail station, the entire place is eerily quiet and abandoned. We linger near the tracks for the better part of fifteen minutes before Adam asks, "What time is it?"

Casper glances at her phone. "Almost five."

He frowns. "It's Saturday."

"Uh huh," Casper says. And then, "Oh—the trains stop running at four on Saturdays."

They look at me as though I should have known this. I hold out my hands helplessly.

"Um... You can stay at my place again, if you want."

"Nope. My folks get home bright and early tomorrow." Casper shifts her bag tiredly from one shoulder to the other. Adam tries to take it from her but she shrugs him off. "Sorry, Vince. Can you drop me off at my house? I'll get you back for gas money."

"Not a big deal." I say this with a little more gusto than is necessary. Because this means she trusts me enough to let me see where she lives. Plus, Adam isn't saying anything. Does that mean he'll come back home with me? We've never spent time alone. Unless Casper sleeping in the next room counts. She naps in my bed while we sit on the balcony and talk about music and movies and things that aren't of great importance.

Would it be different if it were just me and him? Maybe I'd work up the courage to tell him I would miss him, if he were gone. Or that I like his mouth. Or that I'm envious Casper has gotten to hear him sing and I haven't. I could tell him about the email from Harbinger and ask his opinion, see his reaction. Or maybe we'll sit there in uncomfortable silence the entire time without Casper to serve as a buffer for conversation.

It's a bit of a drive to Casper's place, but not nearly as long as if she had to take the light-rail. She lives in a nice neighborhood in a cozy brown house. A nice family home, for her nice family and her nice dog. What would her parents think if they knew she was planning on cutting out early? Would they be upset to lose that time with her? Would it be better for them even if they could never admit it?

"Do you want help with your stuff?" I ask as she pushes open her door. She waves me off.

"I got it. Thanks for the ride and the abundance of food. I think I'm ready to hibernate." A grin crosses her mouth. Then she waves and disappears inside.

I'm alone with Adam.

Adam and I are alone.

Adam is relocating from the back seat, squirming up front into the passenger's seat beside me. We are alone and we're sitting right next to each other. Oh. What is air? How do I breathe again? I swallow hard, forcing back the lump in my throat that is part terror, part excitement.

"Am I taking you home, or did you want to...?"

Adam picks at some lint on his pants. "I don't want to be a bother."

"You're not." Deep breath. "You're never a bother. I'd like it—if you want to, that is. Come back and hang out some more." What am I going for here? I have no idea. Just that I like watching Adam's face, the line of his jaw when he talks, the way he frowns when he's thinking. I wish he smiled more. He has such a nice mouth and it looks even nicer when he smiles.

"If you're sure," he says carefully, casting a sidelong glance in my direction. "I have to stop by home first, if that's okay."

Doesn't make a difference to me. Adam gives me somewhat clumsy directions from Casper's place to his. I say somewhat clumsy, because although he's been to Casper's before (that's news to me) he's always taken a bus and doesn't know the exact streets. Once we hit the freeway, it's smooth sailing.

If Casper's house can be said to be 'cozy,' then Adam's is...grand, I guess. Two stories, with an automatic wrought iron gate that opens with a clicker on his keychain. I vaguely remember a foster home that was this nice from was when I was little. My stay there hadn't lasted long. Inside Adam's house, everything is neatly decorated. Not, like, overdone with classiness or anything, but it's the sort of house you take a look at and know two things. (1) there's a maid that comes regularly and (2) whoever lives here does nothing to accommodate children or animals.

Adam looks out of place with his shaggy black hair and black clothes. But he moves into the house like it's perfectly natural—well, duh, I guess it would be—and leads me into the kitchen. I'm guessing his mom isn't home, or he might've made me stay in the car.

"It's a good thing I didn't see your place before you saw mine," I say quietly, "or I never would've been brave enough to let you come over."

Adam opens a cabinet beneath the sink and pulls out a bag of cat food. "Why are you whispering?"

Oh. "I don't...sorry." I eye the bag of food. "You have a cat?"

"My mom has a cat." He crosses the kitchen to a door leading into the backyard. Everything is gorgeously and meticulously landscaped, with a fenced-in area for the pool, which is as immaculate as the house and sparkles as the setting sun catches on the water. Adam crouches and fills a bowl just outside the door. It, too, looks out of place. As does the scruffy black-and-gray cat that comes darting out of the bushes and shoves its face into Adam's hand.

"From what you've told me"—which isn't much, granted—"your mom doesn't strike me as a cat person."

"She's not." He smiles ruefully, stroking the cat's head and beneath its chin. "Her friend's cat had a litter. Mom thought Crispy was the cutest thing ever and brought him home. I don't know what she was thinking. Guess she didn't realize having a kitten would mean taking it to the vet, feeding it, and cleaning up after it."

"So you do it."

"Someone has to. I keep him outside so she forgets about him, otherwise she'd give him away. But he stays in the back yard and doesn't wander off." He straightens up and steps back inside as Crispy the cat begins devouring his food. "She got bored with her own kid. Not sure why she thought a cat would be different."

I would feel better if Adam sounded sad about that, or even angry. He doesn't. He sounds completely and utterly resigned—because this? This is normal. This is how his life has always been and he's used to it. I hate that. He shouldn't be used to being overlooked and ignored.

"Come on," he says. We go upstairs and to his room at the far end of the hall. It looks nothing like what I expect it to. No posters on the wall, no CDs or records scattered all over the place. Even this space that should belong solely to Adam is clean and model-perfect like the rest of the house. The only thing out of place is a framed, signed photograph of the Beatles hanging to the side of his door. Inconspicuous. Like he's hoping no one notices it's there.

"Holy shit. Is that real?"

"Got it on eBay, so who knows? I think so." He rummages around in his closet for clean clothes. Scruffy hair aside, Adam is always so tidy. He never leaves a mess behind, always does his own dishes, and I've never seen him wear the same outfit. Suddenly I'm self-conscious about the pants I've been wearing for three days straight.

I reach out to touch the frame of the Beatles picture, decide against it, and marvel at it instead. It has to date back to the early sixties, judging by the haircuts. *Help!* era, maybe. Seeing it reminds me of how Adam first approached me with Beatles' lyrics and I turn around, scanning the room, until I spot his computer on his desk (imagining him sitting there by nothing but his tiny desk lamp light, writing to me) and, beside it, his guitar.

"Can I hear you play?"

Adam straightens up from where he was digging out a clean pair of socks. "What?"

"I've never gotten to. Casper talks about it all the time, so..." I gesture at his guitar, hopeful.

He studies me, the guitar, me again, lips drawn tight. "I'm not any good."

"Casper says you are."

"Casper doesn't know music."

"I do."

"Exactly." He turns away. End of conversation.

I don't push him because I wouldn't know how. Besides that, I think I hear a car out front, and a quick look out the window shows a blue SUV pulling into the driveway alongside my crummy old van. "I think your mom is home."

Adam freezes, jaw clenching, and quickly shoves his clothes into his bag. Then he's hurrying me out of the room and downstairs. "Let's get out of here before—"

Mrs Rockswell is just stepping inside when we round the corner for the entryway. She stops in the middle of taking out her earrings. She's pretty. Adam has her cheekbones and nose. She's dressed in office attire, complete with pearls and a red blazer that matches her heels. And she looks as startled to see her son as she does to see me.

"Adam, I thought we'd talked about you having guests over without asking first," she says in a patient, saccharine tone like she's chiding a seven-year-old for not eating his vegetables. I imagine I don't look so hot, standing in her spotless house with my rumpled shirt and three-day-old jeans. I think one of my sneakers is coming untied, too.

"Sorry," Adam mutters. "We were just grabbing some stuff and leaving. Come on, Vince."

I think it might be the first time he's ever directly spoken my name to me. For some reason, it makes heat rush immediately to my face. Would he find it weird if I asked him to say it again?

We start to move around her but Mrs. Rockswell sighs, plucks out her other earring, and gives Adam a withering look. "No, I don't think so."

Adam frowns. "Why not?"

"You didn't ask me about going anywhere."

The look Adam gives her is beyond dubious. "Since when do you care where I go?"

"Watch your attitude, young man." She turns her attention to me, still smiling. "Sorry. Vince, was it?"

"Vincent," I say, because I don't think I like this lady and I don't want her soiling my name when it sounded so nice on Adam's lips a minute ago. "I, um. I can give you my address and all that. If you want. I don't live that far and —"

"No, that's all right." Mrs. Rockswell moves past us, going so far as to tug the packed bag out of Adam's grip. He doesn't relinquish his hold immediately. They stare at each other, and I think they're having this battle of wills wherein neither of them says a word with anything but their eyes.

Mrs. Rockswell wins.

Adam lets go of his bag, but doesn't look at me. "Sorry. Maybe next time."

I'm not sure who's more embarrassed: him for how his mom is acting in front of a friend, or me, for having a friend's mom treat me like I'm dirt. Can't say that I'm not used to it. Corey's parents hated my guts. But I can't help but feel abandoned. This was supposed to be our night to hang out. He's not a kid, so why is he letting his mom push him around?

Unless he never really wanted to go in the first place. Thinking back to our conversation in the car, I wonder if he only agreed because I was being pushy.

So I smile. Thinly, but the effort is there. I say, "Okay. Nice meeting you, Mrs. Rockswell," and I leave without complaint, without argument.

I hope I never have to see that woman again.

From: HARBINGER <admin@yoursuicidewatch.com>

To: NowhereMan <herecomesthesun@beemail.com>

Subject: RE: SW Activity

connections are pointless. they feel great at first. but what happens when the person gets tired of you and decides to leave? it's human nature. people look out for themselves. when they outgrow someone or don't want to be around them, but don't want the drama of dealing with hurt feelings, they brush you off.

everyone is replaceable.

everyone lets you down.

you know,

maybe you and i could

The message cuts off.

Suicide Watch is down. There is no *maintenance being performed* notification, just...a 404 error and that's it. Bizarre. I shoot Casper a text about it, and she calls to say, "*It's been down for a few hours. Who knows? Maybe Harbinger's hosting company realized the kind of site he was running and killed his account.*"

Cut off the website, cut off his email to me but still sent it? I try not to think about it. And I sure as hell won't tell Casper about Harbinger's emails now. So all I really say is, "Oh, weird."

"*Weird, yeah.*" Her voice is off. Like there's something she isn't telling me. "*Isn't Adam with you?*"

My stomach flip-flops. "No. I took him home. Why?"

"*Are you kidding? Please tell me you're kidding.*"

"Why would I be?" Should I tell her about Adam's crazy mom? I wonder if she's seen his house. If they've met. I can't picture Casper keeping her mouth shut if Mrs. Rockswell tried removing her from the premises. She also would've told Adam off for not having a spine.

"*Because I totally gave up my night out so you two would have some alone time,*" she says, exasperated.

"But you said your parents were coming home."

"*They are. Tomorrow night.*"

I run a hand through my hair, sighing heavily.

"Okay. Do I want to know what the point of that was, then? Giving us alone time?"

Casper bites back a laugh. *"Oh, come on, Vinny. Do you think I don't see how you look at him? I'm always half a second away from telling you to wipe the drool off your face."*

My cheeks burn with the onslaught of blood to my face. "It's not like that. He's—I don't even know if he's..."

"Gay?"

"That's sort of...you know, important to having...something...happen." I don't even know what I'm trying to say. My tongue is in knots and my words aren't translating between my brain and my mouth correctly.

"To be honest, I don't think Adam classifies things like that. He likes you. He trusts you."

As much as I want to delve deeper into the subject of Adam liking and/or trusting me, I don't say a word. I can't. I've never been involved with anyone. I mean, I've kissed one guy at a party with Corey (or should I say, he kissed me), but that was years ago and nothing ever came of it. Nothing good, anyway. Nothing beyond getting shoved into a dumpster after school, or having my head held underwater during gym swim lessons.

"I have to go," I mutter.

"Vincent, don't be like that."

But I am. So I say goodnight and hang up.

SUICIDE WATCH

CHAPTER 16

Adam emails me an apology later: *sorry about mom.* I don't respond because my feelings are still hurt, and it's probably stupid, but I can't help but feel betrayed. He's eighteen. His mom doesn't have a right to order him around anymore.

Then again, I didn't listen much to anyone growing up. I didn't listen to my older foster siblings, not to my foster parents, not to teachers at school. That isn't to say I was some kind of rebel who purposely broke the rules, but if the rules were something I *really* didn't want to do...

Like oral reports. Who the hell thought it was a great idea to take a kid who all the other kids hate, put him at the front of the class, and expect him to give a presentation without breaking down into tears? I tried it once, in middle school. Never again. That would account for part of my miserable grades.

"Vincent has potential, but he does not get along well when working in groups or participating in class."

There's a difference between not participating and working well in groups, and knowing it's smarter not to because the other kids will torment you. I've been thrown into so many lockers and garbage cans, chased home, had my lunch stolen, and my shoes yanked off my feet—laces tied together and tossed over power lines—to last me a lifetime.

So who cares if I didn't want to make an idiot out of myself in front of my classes? Who cares if I wanted to draw rabbits and people in art, instead of a bowl of fruit? Who cares if I can't sleep and want to go for a walk at two in the morning?

But I never hurt anyone—unless they hurt me first, physically or emotionally. Even then I wasn't much of a fighter so I doubt I did any real damage. I wasn't intentionally mean to anyone. I tried to focus in class, even if I didn't get it, or I was too distracted with the thoughts in my own head.

I didn't mean to be a bad kid. I swear, I didn't.

I just wanted a little control in my life. Little acts of defiance were the only way I achieved that.

Maggie understood, to a degree. We got into our arguments, but as long as I worked hard and I was honest she didn't try to keep me from doing the things that made me happy. She let me go jogging in the middle of the night, so long as she knew the route I was taking and I had my phone. She took me out of high school and let me enroll in independent study where I could move at my own pace and catch up on the stuff I'd failed the few years prior.

All parents should be more like her. Less like Adam's mom. All kids should be more willing to fight for the privilege to have some sort of freedom instead of being on a ball and chain all the time.

I don't write Adam back because I don't know what to say and I have no idea if I'm being irrational. I am when I'm upset, Corey used to say. So it's better to keep my mouth shut until I'm done being mad and can pretend nothing happened.

Which might work except Adam calls the next day, which isn't nearly enough time for me to get over it. Maybe I should've responded to the email and said something, anything, to appease him so he'd leave me alone.

Or maybe I didn't *want* him to leave me alone. Maybe I wanted to see if he'd call. I don't know. But some part of me is thrilled when his number shows up on my phone. Adam doesn't want to upset me. Adam cares enough about my feelings that he wants to make sure we're okay. My heart is pounding.

"Hello?"

"*Hey.*"

I wipe my palms against my jeans, phone cradled between shoulder and cheek. "Hi. Um, how are you?"

"*I'm all right.*" Pause. "*I wasn't sure if you got my email and...yeah, you know. Sorry. About the other day. I don't know what got into her.*"

"No, it's fine." It wasn't fine five minutes ago, but the second I heard Adam's voice it *became* fine. Something to think about.

"*If it were fine, you would've written me back,*" Adam says, a hint of uncertainty creeping into his voice.

Caught.

"It *is* fine now. I mean...it's not like anyone's parents have ever liked me, I just..."

"*Just?*"

My turn to pause, letting the silence hang on the line between us. "I don't get it, is all. You could have told her off."

"*She's my mom, Vince. I can't just 'tell her off.'*"

"Sure you can."

Adam doesn't respond. I picture him perched on the edge of his bed like I am, slouching where my back is ramrod straight, picking non-existent lint off his hoodie. Silent because silence and Adam are the best of friends. It drives me crazy. After an eternity he says, almost timidly, almost incoherent because he's mumbling, "*What about next weekend? If you want to...hang out or whatever.*"

Deep breath, Vincent. "What if she says no then?"

"*She won't be in town. She's leaving on Thursday.*"

"So it would be a secret." Oh, that rubs me the wrong way. Corey did the same thing, hiding just how much time she spent with me from her parents because they thought I was a bad influence. Casper does that, because her parents would never let her leave the house with a pair of boys they wouldn't trust to take care of her. I've never *liked* being some dirty little secret, but I've always understood it—until now. Coming from Adam, it hurts more. "We'll just hang out when your mom's out of town and when she's around, we'll be careful not to let her in on it, is that right?"

"*It's not that big a deal. It's just...easier this way.*"

I try to regroup my thoughts. "It *is* a big deal. It's not like she was asking you to do your homework or take out the trash. She didn't have a legitimate reason for telling you no other than she didn't want you hanging out with me. I mean, if she's never home anyway, what's it to her where you are or who you're with? Whether she's your mom or not—"

"*You don't have parents,*" Adam snaps, "*so don't pretend you know what it's like.*"

It's a big helping of cold water dumped over my head. I stare at the wall and try to figure out if he just said what I think he said.

Adam draws in a breath. His voice hitches.

"*Vince. I'm sorr —* "

I hang up.

I medicate myself for the next five days to keep from feeling.

October

SUICIDE WATCH

CHAPTER 17

My turntable is cranked up as loud as I think my neighbors will let me get away with. Lying on the floor with my eyes closed and George Harrison singing in my ear means I don't hear Casper calling repeatedly. It's not until almost two in the morning, when I finally figure I ought to get some sleep, that I notice I have four missed calls and a barrage of texts. She says it's urgent. I'm tired, my mind is foggy from the medication, and I don't care.

I hate this medicine. Or I would, if I had the energy to. No longer am I mad at Adam, or frustrated with myself. I'm...

Just.

Here.

Going to bed. Will text in the AM., I write to Casper

No sooner have I slipped off my shirt and collapsed into bed than she's texted back: *No. Talk now.*

I don't have a chance to respond before she's calling. Arguing with Casper would probably take more energy than answering the damn phone and hearing whatever she wants to say, so I sigh, roll onto my side, and tuck the phone between my ear and the pillow. "Shouldn't you be sleeping?"

"*Dude, you have to get on your computer and see the email I just sent you.*"

"It's two in the morning, Casper. I'm going to sleep."

She sounds positively giddy. "*Suicide Watch is gone. The cops shut it down and Harbinger is being investigated.*"

That gets my attention, even if I'm not sure what I feel about it beyond a tiny seed of anxiety nestling in the pit of my stomach. "What?"

"*A family of one of the members who offed themselves found the site in his internet history and reported it. They're investigating because there are a lot of minors registered."*

I run a hand over my face, trying to clear my head. What a time for me to be out of it. "They can't arrest someone for having a forum for people who want to die."

"No, but they can arrest someone for assisting suicide. Just because he didn't pull the trigger or give them the pills, he still went into it with the knowledge of what they planned to do and didn't phone for help afterward."

The photos, I remember. We talked about Harbinger being there with some of those people when they died. Then it dawns on me—

"Joey?"

Casper is silent but I can hear her breathing.

It suddenly makes sense why Casper freaked out when Joey died. Why she sounded so distant when the website first went down. Why she's so excited now. "I'm not sure if I'm following. Harbinger was there? How do you know?"

"Because he posted the picture. That was how I found out Joey was gone. He's spent the last month telling me he was doing better, that he thought he wanted to hang in there a bit longer. He wasn't ready to go, Vince. Then suddenly, out of nowhere, Harbinger arranges a meeting with him and Joey's dead? It makes no sense."

No. It doesn't.

My insides are so cold. Is that what Harbinger does? Talks people into offing themselves? Joey was from the Chicago area. The more I think about it, so were the other members whose photos were taken by Harbinger. Either they lived in Chicago or they were within driving distance from it.

It's possible he hasn't just been witnessing suicides, he's been *helping* them.

Then I think about Jessica and I wonder if that makes me no better than Harbinger. I could've grabbed her, could've stopped her. I was close enough. But all I did was ask her name and watch as she flung herself into oblivion.

I would laugh if I wasn't so close to crying.

I wanted so desperately to feel *something* when Maggie died, and now I'm feeling entirely too much. There is no happy medium.

"Does that mean anything for us, do you think? They have our information, but it's not like...they have names and numbers."

"*Don't know. They have IP addresses. They could track everyone if they really wanted, but I guess the question is...how important is it? They're more likely to go after minors.*"

I pause. "You're seventeen."

"*Good thing I'll probably be dead before they get around to finding me, huh?*" She sounds genuinely amused by this fact. I am going to be sick.

I blink back the blurriness in my eyes. "I hate it when you say things like that."

"*You didn't used to.*"

"I didn't used to care."

"*You care that you're going to lose a friend, and it will hurt. But whether I kill myself or not, you're going to lose me either way. You're going to have to deal with it.*"

It's true. And I hate it.

Some stupid, baser part of my mind keeps thinking that if I can make Casper happy, if I can be her friend, then she won't die. What a stupid thought. She is unfixable. I close my eyes and try to tell myself it's no failing of mine and no one else would be able to save her either.

Casper takes my silence for only a few seconds more before sighing in exasperation. "*God, I'm so sick of this house. Come get me?*"

I pull the phone back to glance at the time. "It's almost three in the morning."

"*Got anything better to do?*"

"Well, no. What about your parents?"

"*Sleeping. I can sneak out.*"

She's going to get me arrested for kidnapping. Great. I'm also not sure if I should be driving while I'm medicated, but I sigh, run a hand over my face, and roll out of bed. "Okay. All right. Let me wake up a bit and I'll be on my way."

I park across the street from Casper's house. My eyes burn with the want to sleep. In fact, I'm almost considering laying my head against the steering wheel and dozing off when I see Casper creeping around the side of the house. She spots the van and trots across the road, climbs in beside me, and lets out a heavy puff of air. "See, no problems."

"And where will they think you are when they get up in a few hours?" I ask, cranking up the heat because Casper looks tiny and cold, huddled in the worn seat.

"Just drive." She presses her hands to a vent and closes her eyes. "I deleted my email account."

The van pulls away from the curb, turning around to head back the way I came. A frown creases my brow. "Why would you do that?"

"Seemed like a good idea. Just in case anyone tries to contact me about Suicide Watch. I mean, I want to see Harbinger rot in jail for what he did to Joey, so I've saved everything. But I'm not sure I feel up to dealing with all the drama just yet. Can you imagine how well that would go over with my parents? Them finding out I've been chatting people up on a pro-suicide forum? Maybe it doesn't help much, but I can make a new account."

"Oh." Pause. I wonder if something interrupted Harbinger mid-email to me. Automatic reaction: hit send before someone sees your screen. "Maybe I should do that, too."

"And Adam. We need to let him know."

My frown deepens. Casper notices.

"Come off it, Vinny. Is it really worth still being pissed off with him?"

I grumble a non-committal answer. She jabs a finger into my ribs, which in turn makes me jerk the wheel to the left. I'm ticklish, dammit.

"Jesus, Casper—"

She bites back a laugh. "That's what you get for not talking to me. You have to talk to someone."

Maybe, yeah. I should. But not to the dying girl. She has enough to deal with. "It doesn't matter. I'll get over it."

"You're making the assumption that you being irrational is totally acceptable behavior," Casper drawls, toying with the buttons on the radio to find a station. "Maybe in a week, two weeks, you'll get over it. But what if he doesn't? You two are both so fucking oversensitive about everything."

Tension slithers up my spine. My jaw tightens. "I'm allowed to be angry."

"Of course you are. Emotions are totally irrational half the time." Her ice blue eyes lock onto me. "But you have full control over how you *deal* with them. Acknowledging that something is irrational and refraining from taking it out on someone is the best thing to do."

I am silent.

I am panicking. What if she's right and he doesn't forgive me for overreacting?

"You need to realize Adam didn't ditch you, Vinny. He's got his own set of issues, mostly pertaining to his mom. You happened to be caught in the middle of it. How do you think Adam felt after you left? Stuck with his mom while she berated him about his choice of friends and told him to go to his room like he's a five-year-old?"

I can picture it, but I don't want to. Adam, sitting quietly in his room, on the edge of his bed. Maybe wanting to play his guitar, but not daring to try because his mother might flip out about the noise. If we'd gone only ten minutes earlier we would have slipped out of the house before she came home.

"I'll call him," I mutter. Mostly just to get her off my case.

Casper is placated for the moment. We head home and she manages a small bowl of cereal before we both crawl into bed and sleep.

CHAPTER 18

The trees are turning orange and gold outside my window and the air has a fun autumn-y scent. It's the first day I haven't taken my medicine in a week and a half, and I'm feeling human again. Shaky, a little crazy, but less robotic.

(I've called Adam three times.)

I celebrate that evening by turning *I Want to Break Free* on loud, opening the sliding glass door to let in the cool air, and clean.

(He hasn't called back.)

I vacuum and shove laundry into the tiny stackable washer and dryer in the hall closet. I scrub the bathroom and mop the kitchen. Maggie used to nag me to get these things done around her house, and I feel a little more adult-like that I'm doing it in my own apartment because I want to and not because I have to.

(I've emailed and texted. If I think about it too much I'm going to have to medicate again.)

Casper had planned on coming over tonight, but backed out at the last minute saying she wasn't feeling so hot. This marks the very first time she's cancelled plans on me, and I might've freaked out over it had the exhaustion in her voice not been so evident.

But she calls just as I'm finishing up the kitchen, and she tells me she slept all day and now she's not going to be able to sleep tonight. My hands smell like cleaner. I wipe them on my jeans and sink down onto the bed, popping open my laptop. Nothing more has happened with Suicide Watch, but I keep an eye on the news just the same.

I saved all the emails from Harbinger.

Just in case.

I don't know what I'll do with them.

"I've been cleaning," I tell Casper.

"*Glad to know my absence promotes productivity.*" Casper yawns. "*Seriously. I think I'm gonna try to get back to sleep. Screwing up my sleep schedule is so not okay and the internet is boring tonight.*"

"Hold up." I hold the phone between my cheek and shoulder so my right hand is free to maneuver the touchpad, my heart doing acrobatics in my throat. "I have an email from Adam."

"*Oh, weird. So do I.*"

We're both silent while we read. Eventually Casper scoffs and sighs, "*Just lyrics.*"

In My Life. I told Adam in an email once it was one of my favorite Beatles songs and he agreed it was one of his, too. I don't ask Casper if she got the same email as I did, because something is off.

(Three calls, four emails, two texts. No response.)

I know these lyrics like I know my own name. There's a wrong line. And maybe this is a stupid thing to notice, but I do notice, because this is *Adam* and how would Adam of all people, with his meticulous attention to detail and his love of The Beatles, ever get a word wrong in one of their songs?

But *some are dead and some are living* has suddenly become *some are dead and some are dying* and the only person in Adam's life who would notice he changed something so stupid and seemingly insignificant on purpose is...

I can't breathe.

"*You still there? What's wrong?*"

"I have to go," is all I manage, sliding off the bed. "Call 911. Adam's going to do it." Is doing it. Has done it.

Oh.

God.

I am...

CHAPTER 19

I throw myself behind the wheel of the van and tear off for the freeway to Adam's house. If it weren't for my last visit, I wouldn't have remembered the way. I could have gotten lost. I could have forgotten which house it was. As it is, what if I'm driving too slowly? What if I'm too late?

What if.

What if.

The automatic gates are already open because there are two ambulances outside, lights flashing red, red, red. I pull up as one of them is leaving, sirens blaring high and loud and urgent.

I will never breathe again if something has happened to Adam.

All I can do is hope Casper's phone call got them here in time. That we weren't too slow. That the thirty seconds it took me to figure out Adam's message wasn't twenty seconds too long.

I stumble out of the van to where a police cruiser is parked; an officer is calling in on his radio. He stops to look at me, eyebrows raised.

"Where did they take him?" My voice comes out surprisingly steady. Funny, considering I'm about to tremble to pieces. When the officer doesn't respond immediately I say, more urgently, "Where did they take Adam? I'm his friend. We called in that something was wrong."

The cop pulls off his hat, scratches a hand through his short hair, a thoughtful look on his face. "They're taking him to Mercy Ridge, off of Ninth and L."

Ninth and L. I don't know where the hell that is in this neighborhood, but I jump back into the car without so much as a thank you, and Google the hospital so my GPS can read me the directions.

I get there in one piece. Without getting lost. I go in through the ER entrance because I have no idea where else to go. The last time I stepped foot inside a hospital, they told me Maggie was dead. Now are they going to tell me Adam is dead? That it's pointless for someone like me to get attached to anything because we are all broken and Adam is gone and soon Casper will be, too?

The sleepy-looking nurse behind the receptionist's desk is less than impressed when I budge in front of a mother and her squalling infant to ask, "Where do I go if I want to see a patient?" Despite her sullen glare, she points me in the direction of a set of double doors where I find another desk, with another receptionist, who only looks at me when I tell him I'm searching for the boy who was just brought in—Adam Rockswell.

He looks over the tops of his glasses. "Are you family?"

"Yes." The lie comes easily. I knew they would ask me. If I were to tell the truth, they wouldn't let me in, and they sure as hell wouldn't keep me updated on his condition. Also a good thing this guy obviously hasn't seen Adam, because he'd know there's no way we're related. Me with my olive-skin tone and brown curls. Adam with his pale complexion, big gold eyes, and fine, straight dark hair. A blind man couldn't mistake us for brothers.

The guy picks up his phone to make a call and asks for a status on Rockswell. When he hangs up, his tone is a little more kind. "Sorry, but the doctors are working on him."

I brace my hands against the counter, certain my legs are going to give out. "What did he...will he be..."

"Sorry, son. It's too early to tell." He shrugs, but it isn't unkind, more with the tired sympathy of someone who sees this sort of thing day in and day out. "Might want to bunker down for a bit. I'll let you know as soon as I hear anything."

I think I say thank you, but I'm not sure if the sound

makes it past my throat. Bunker down, huh? What other choice do I have?

Across from his desk is an alcove with a TV, vending machine, a couple of chairs, and stacks of magazines. If this were the hospital Maggie was taken to, the magazines would be a year old and the TV would be static-y. But this is a hospital in the nice side of town so of course everything is shiny and new. All I can hope is their doctors are worth the money they're paid because they will be the difference between whether Adam lives or dies.

I don't know how long I sit there. Several sitcoms, a few talk shows. Three volumes of Cosmo, read front to back. I even do the crossword on a newspaper. There is no reception for me to call Casper and let her know what's happening, and I'm afraid if I step outside I'll miss something vital. Besides, I tell myself, I have no news to report to her yet. She's as much in the dark as I am.

The guy at the desk isn't even there anymore. He's been replaced by an elderly gentleman with coke-bottle glasses and a smoker's cough. I accost him almost immediately, feeling drained but no less nauseated. I tried stomaching a Pepsi from the vending machine, but the idea of food is too much.

"Excuse me. Can you call up and see if there's a status update on Adam Rockswell?"

He calls, tries to make idle chatter until a doctor comes down. The doctor gives me a bewildered smile as he offers his hand. "So you're his...brother."

He, obviously, has seen Adam. I shake his hand dumbly, because I don't know what else to do, but I say "Step-brother," in hopes it will alleviate his suspicion.

"Of course. I'm Doctor Carl. First, let me just say that Adam should be fine."

All the air has dropped out of me. I lean against the counter. Shut my eyes. Gingerly scoop up the pieces of my heart and mush them back together like play-dough.

He'll be okay.

"Can I see him?"

Doctor Carl leads me through a door I've seen others go through only when the guy behind the desk buzzed them through. I have to wear a nametag that says *Visitor* across the top. Just visiting. No worries. I won't keel over and die on your floors, because Adam is going to be okay.

As we walk, the hallways, nurses, doctors, patients, all blurring around me, Doctor Carl explains the pills Adam took dropped his blood pressure significantly, so they gave him stuff to counteract it. It had started to seep into his bloodstream, but they got to him in time before it could do any significant damage to his liver or kidneys.

As we stop outside a patient room, he says, "Adam isn't breathing entirely on his own just yet, so we're keeping him on a ventilator. Just until he wakes up." Before I can nod and step inside, he touches my arm. "Vincent... Can you think of any reason Adam would want to kill himself?"

I stare at him, because there are a thousand reasons. Like how his dad is dead and his mom would rather he didn't exist and he thinks he's all alone in the world, even though he's not, because he has me—for however little that's worth—and if anything happened to him...

I say: "He's had a rough time lately."

Doctor Carl nods. "We'll have to keep him for a few days for observation and to have a psych evaluate his mental state. We've only just got in touch with your mother when she arrived at her hotel. She won't be back until tomorrow, so perhaps you could keep her updated in the meantime."

Oh. Mrs Rockswell left for one of her business trips, right? The thought pisses me off. She and Adam must've gotten into some kind of argument before she left. He would've been upset and alone, and now...now she isn't even here when he needs her most.

I nod again and step into the dimly lit room. The hiss

of machines — the ventilator, I guess — sets me on edge. Adam will not wake up alone, even if I have to sleep on the floor next to his bed. How scary would that be? Opening your eyes with a tube down your throat in a cold, sterile-smelling room, IVs, and patients in various other parts of the ER shouting or crying. Hospitals are not quiet. They are not peaceful. They are not conducive to positive mental health.

Like I'd know anything about that.

I nudge aside the curtains that have been drawn around Adam's bed. He's asleep, yes. Looking small, pale, and fragile against the starched sheets. There's the ventilator mask over his mouth and I hate it. He would hate it.

He doesn't respond when I stop at the foot of his bed and place a hand on his leg through the blankets. I'm unsure if he can hear me, if he *wants* to hear me. For the first time, it dawns on me that maybe Adam will be angry at Casper and me for calling an ambulance. We've fucked up his chance at getting out of a life he hated. Did we have that right? At the time, I was positive of what I was doing. *Save Adam.*

Now, I'm not so sure.

"Hey." Even a whisper sounds so deafening in this cave. "Adam, it's me. Can you hear me?" Like he can answer. I put on my big-boy pants for the courage to move up to Adam's side. I've spent a lot of time staring at him before, but it's different when I don't have to worry about him catching me in the act.

Adam has beautiful hands, one of which I take in mine as I sit in a chair at his bedside. His fingers are long, slightly calloused at the tips from guitar playing. I trace the pad of my thumb over the fine bones in the back of his hand, over his knuckles, down each finger to where he's bitten his nails short.

"You might be mad at me when you wake up," I say as I continue my study of his hand, his wrist, his arm. Easier than looking at his face and wanting to cry. "I'm sorry. That you'll be mad, I mean. I'm not sorry I called for help."

SUICIDE WATCH

    For half a second, the machine monitoring Adam's heart catches, the rhythm momentarily disturbed. Then it returns to normal. I wish I knew if every rise and fall of his chest was his own, or simply powered by the ventilator.

    "Look. I know you think life is terrible. And it is. It's...pretty shitty, actually. But you weren't supposed to do this. Not yet. You think it's fine, because no one would really miss you, but you're wrong."

    My voice hitches, cracks.

    "You're really, really wrong, Adam. *I* would miss you."

CHAPTER 20

There's a blanket around my shoulders when I wake up. No idea when or how it got there. I have a crick in my neck and back from sleeping hunched over in the chair, arms as a pillow on the bed. Adam looks no different. Maybe paler with the sunlight coming through his window. It makes my head hurt. What woke me up was a nurse standing on the opposite side of Adam, checking his vitals. I assume that's what she's doing, anyway. Her name tag reads Monica.

When she notices me sitting up, she winks. "Good morning. You were out like a light."

I rub at my eyes. "What time is it?"

"A little after ten." She tucks her clipboard under her arm. "How about some breakfast?"

Last night, the thought of food was enough to make me hurl. Now, though... I think it's been nearly twenty-four hours since I last ate. So I nod mutely.

Monica the nurse comes back with a tray of food. Nothing spectacular, but I see she's snagged an extra pudding cup for me, and although the eggs and toast are cold they don't taste half bad. I eat in silence, stealing the occasional look at Adam, feeling guilty I'm eating a breakfast he can't enjoy.

After I'm done, I sit back and pull my legs to my chest, just watching him breathe. Watching him sleep. Watching him, I hope, heal.

His eyelids flutter.

It's so brief, I'm certain I imagined it. But it makes me lean forward all the same, and a moment later, the gesture is repeated. Adam shifts slowly, subtly, lifting a hand a few inches from the bed with a choked, confused sound.

I'm on my feet and jabbing at the nurse's button

before taking his hand.

"Shh, Adam. Hey. Hi. It's okay; don't freak out..."

His eyes slide open a fraction of an inch, blurry and tired and, yes, a bit afraid. I don't have time to do anything beyond smile at him, because there's a *click click* of heels which I assume to be Monica but, in fact, belong to Adam's mother.

Oh.

Mrs. Rockswell is poised in the doorway.

Our eyes lock. We stay right where we are until Monica bursts in, nearly shoving Mrs. Rockswell into the doorjamb with a quick apology.

"Is he awake?" Monica asks. I nod. At least, I think I do. My eyes haven't left Mrs. Rockswell's. Monica speaks low, soothing words to Adam. Something about it seems to snap his mom out of her daze.

"I thought only family were allowed in here," she says icily.

Monica only briefly glances up. "Well, yes, he's..." She glances at me, mouth open. Realization sets in. "...We made an exception, seeing as no one else was here for him."

I could hug her.

Mrs. Rockswell steps away from the door. Monica no longer seems to exist in her sphere of things to care about. "I want you to listen to me. Adam has never, *ever* had any sort of problems until he started hanging around *you*. Then he magically develops a habit for shouting and talking back to his mother? I don't know what garbage you're getting him involved with, but it's unacceptable. Please leave. *Now.*"

The last thing in the world I can picture is soft-spoken Adam shouting, but it's a funny image. I might laugh if I didn't hate this woman so much. "He's always had these problems and you never paid attention. He's been unhappy for a long time, because you don't care about him, and his dad didn't care about him, then his dad died and you didn't even *pretend* to care except when he spilled jam on your carpets and ruined your stupid parties!"

Adam's grip on my hand tightens. I think. I can't be sure. I must be squeezing the blood out of his poor fingers.

"You have ten seconds to get out of here before I call security and have you *thrown* out," she says quietly, an underlying anger simmering beneath the surface. She looks ready to hit me. I wish she would. Then we would see who'd be getting thrown out of the hospital. I bet Monica would take my side.

But I don't want to put her in that position. I don't want *Adam* upset. He's already staring at me with wide, round, frightened eyes that still aren't quite all there, so I disentangle my hand from his after one last squeeze, and march for the door. Hoping Adam doesn't hate me. Hoping his mom doesn't make him regret that we saved his life.

If I ever go to their house again, I'm dumping jam all over her carpets.

SUICIDE WATCH

CHAPTER 21

Adam's ok. Will call later, is all I text to Casper during the hour I'm sitting outside the animal shelter, waiting for it to open. As soon as the doors unlock, I push past a few others who were lingering and head straight for the kennels.

Today's dog is a fat Pit-bull named Roger. I scratch under his chin through the fence. He's so massive that when he rolls onto his back, he has a hard time getting up again. He's ugly and he drools a lot, but I want him to find a home. He'd make some family so happy if they'd only see how sweet he is.

I shuffle out of the shelter, not sure if I feel better or worse for my visit. My phone has been going off the hook with Casper's texts and missed calls that it's vibrated itself right off the seat and onto the floorboard. I retrieve it and call her back with a sigh.

"*I'm going to fucking kill you. What took so long?*"

"Sorry," I mumble. "I was... I got distracted. Adam should be okay."

"*Did he wake up? Did you talk to him?*"

"No. Yes. Sort of? His mom showed up just as he was starting to come to. She kicked me out."

"*God, that woman...*" Casper sighs. It's a heavy, tired sound. She's feeling worse. "*Come over for a bit and fill me in on everything?*"

Pause. "Come over as in...come over. To your place. And hang out?"

"*Um, yeah. That's what I said.*"

I chew at the inside of my cheek. "What about your parents?"

"*Mom's at work and Dad's here, but he'll probably head out to run some errands. And who cares? They won't have a problem with you being here.*"

I relent and say I'll be there soon. It isn't until I'm driving for Casper's that I realize there has to be a reason Casper has never had Adam and me over before, and that this means she wants to see me, but she isn't feeling well enough to leave the house.

She's getting sicker, and I didn't even ask how she was feeling.

There's a car in front of Casper's house when I pull up. I scrub my palms against my pants before knocking on the front door, worried her dad will answer and I'll be known as the smelly dog guy.

Thankfully, it's Casper who pulls open the door. It's only been a week since I saw her last, but under her eyes are dark and her cheeks are more hollow than I remember. She grins as she steps aside, beckoning me in. I'm praying under my breath her house isn't as immaculate as Adam's, or that her dad isn't as terrifying and infuriating as Mrs. Rockswell.

Nothing to worry about. Immediately, I'm more at home here than I was at Adam's. There are shoes piled just inside the door. Sneakers, work boots, a pair of heels. Casper is in her socks so I hesitate, but she rolls her eyes, takes my hand, and drags me out of the entryway.

"Don't worry. You can ditch your shoes wherever."

Not at all like Adam's. Not even like my apartment. I hate people wearing shoes in my place. I let Casper lead me to her room, past the kitchen and a bathroom. No sign of anyone else. Maybe the car in the driveway doesn't mean anything?

Her bedroom is about half the size of my entire apartment. Which isn't to say it's huge, but it's bigger than the room I had at Maggie's. Kind of messy, too. Books lying around — I resist the urge to put them on her bookshelf in alphabetical order — overflowing laundry basket, and shoes here and there. Casper is, obviously, a shoe person.

She sinks onto the unmade bed, tucking her socked feet under the sheet and blankets. Her pajamas look like they used to fit her better, once upon a time, before she became so small. "So...what happened?"

I'm distracted wandering her room, looking around, studying all the things about Casper she's never told me. "I got there just as they were taking him to the hospital," I say absently, coming to a halt in front of her mirrored closet door where photographs are taped around the edges. Smiling faces of people I don't know. I don't recognize Casper. Not at first.

She was right; she used to be fuller-figured, with a round face and shapely hips. Honestly, the weight looks nice on her. Now she's all bones held together by skin. I touch my fingers to a picture. Casper is standing next to a boy who looms over her, but he has a huge grin on his face and an arm around her shoulders. Boyfriend, I'd guess.

"Did you stay there all night?"

My hand falls away. I turn around. "I couldn't leave him there alone. What if he woke up?"

Casper tilts her head, hands clasped loosely atop her knees. "But he didn't. Not until his mom showed up."

I stare at her, unblinking. "Do you think he's going to hate us?"

"Maybe." Shrug. "Does it matter?"

"Of course it matters. What if he never talks to us again?" I almost say *me*. What if he never talks to *me* again? But this isn't about just me, and if Adam is pissed at one of us he'll be pissed at us both.

"And if he hadn't made it, we wouldn't ever talk to him again anyway. I wouldn't say we'll be missing anything except the guilt of thinking we let our best friend die." She raises an eyebrow, and is completely right.

"Why'd we do it, though?" I push my hands through my hair, fingers clutching at the curls like I could, might, rip them out in clumps. "He wanted to die. He always said planning your suicide is stupid like if he ever did it, he wouldn't give any warning, right? It would be a spur of the moment kind of thing."

Casper sighs, sinking back against her pillows, shifting like she can't get comfortable even in her own bed. She presses a hand against her abdomen. "*I* did it because it would've been a shame."

"A shame?"

"You guys don't get it, do you?" She fixes her gaze on the ceiling. "You have forever. You have a *choice*."

My hands drop to my sides.

"There are all these shitty things, and you feel alone, and you feel sad, and sometimes the sadness is this all-encompassing...*thing*, this monster that eats you from the inside out. Not existing is the less painful alternative. But you and Adam have the rest of your lives to make things better and find happiness, you know?"

The rest of our lives, she says. How long will that be? I sink onto the bed beside her.

Casper doesn't look at me. "You saved him because you've got a thing for him. He's like you. Broken, but fixable."

I stare at my hands while Casper stares at nothing and for a few minutes we sit like that, because there's no point in trying to deny the things she knows and I won't insult her by trying to lie. Instead I say, quietly, "I don't want you to go."

"It's going to happen."

My voice catches. "How do you...do it? Worry about other peoples' problems when..."

"What else is there for me to worry about? I don't want to keep dwelling on death and dying." She sighs. "I don't have a lot of time. But I have an awful lot of regrets. The most I can do is make sure I don't leave behind a mess I could've helped clean up. I want you and Adam to be taken care of."

From the corner of my eyes, I catch sight of the pill bottles on her nightstand. Pain medications? I don't know. I'm afraid to. But I have to know something, some kind of details. "What kind of cancer is it?"

Casper actually glances at me, like she's surprised I grew a pair long enough to ask. "Cervical."

Cervical cancer. Not something I know anything about, so I say, "Oh."

"I started getting these back and leg pains. Stopped eating, lost weight." She smiles distantly. "Cervical cancer doesn't have many symptoms until it spreads. That's why a Gyno checks for it. They even have vaccinations for it now. Except I'd never gotten around to going in for a routine checkup, and then I ignored the symptoms for so long that by the time I did get seen, the cancer had gotten into all the organs below my lungs." She shrugs and closes her eyes. "I got a complete hysterectomy. Ovaries, uterus, the whole shebang. Underwent radiation, cryotherapy, chemo. But it wasn't enough. My parents blame themselves for not making me go in sooner. I really think it doesn't matter. Everything had to happen in just the right way for it to have become fatal. If it's anyone's fault, it's mine for ignoring the signs."

Without thinking, I reach out to grab her hand. It's small and thin and birdlike in my grip, but I want...something. A kind of contact. Reassurance that this isn't her fault because how could she have possibly known? Reassurance to myself that, at least for now, she's here and alive and I ought to cherish that.

Casper stares at our joined hands for a long while, expressionless, before she shifts her hand in order to wrap her fingers around mine in return. She curls into me, tucked against my side, and lays her head on my shoulder.

I turn to murmur against her short hair, "I'm afraid."
"Of what? Living? It's not so bad."

```
SUICIDE WATCH
```

"No. I'm afraid of you going away."

Casper sighs. I can't see her face. "Yeah," she whispers. "So am I."

CHAPTER 22

When Casper's dad steps into the room, Casper is fast asleep.

He's a tall guy with a beard and mustache, but both are close-cut, neatly trimmed, like for an office setting. He seems out of place in a t-shirt and jeans. Probably more at home in button-up shirts, ties, and slacks. Come to think of it, I have no clue what Casper's parents do for a living.

He stops in the doorway and stares at us. Casper is curled up against me, sleeping away, and I've spent the last thirty minutes studying the ceiling like I'm now studying her dad and hoping he doesn't rip me a new one for finding me in bed with his daughter.

"She's sleeping," I say lamely, as though he can't already see that for himself. I untangle myself and slowly get up, rather glad I didn't doze off, too. Nothing says *awkward* like waking up to a girl's dad glaring down at you.

Casper's dad tips his head. "I'm Robert, Caitlin's dad. You must be Vincent."

At first I think *he knows me!* And then I think *shit, he knows me*, because I have no clue *how* he knows me or what Casper might have said. Then I think, *her real name is Caitlin and I should have known that by now.*

I stiffly take the hand he offers. "Yeah. Sorry, we were just...talking. And I mean, we talking in the sense that we were *actually* talking and not..." God, Vincent, shut up.

He cracks a smile, gives my hand a squeeze, draws back, and gestures for the door. We step into the hall so we don't disturb Casper. "I've met Adam already, so I figured you had to be the other friend she's been sneaking out with."

I freeze. Instantly my mind begins running through the consequences the two of us could be facing for helping Casper sneak out of her house. She's still seventeen, a minor, and her parents know she's been sneaking out to sleep at my place. "You...know about that?"

"I do now."

Oh, shit.

Robert gives a soft laugh and leads me down the hall. "Don't look like I've just sentenced you to death. We know she's been sneaking out, but..."

"You don't feel like you should punish her?" I ask, and instantly wonder if I shouldn't keep my mouth shut.

"Guess that's about right." He glances at me. "Like I said, we've met Adam a few times. Seems like a good kid. Is he a good kid?"

I think of Adam at the hospital right now, needing a machine to help him breathe. I swallow the lump in my throat and nod. "Yes, sir."

"And are you a good kid?"

The question catches me off-guard. Am I? I don't know. Maggie said I was, but she was the only one. She said I was good, just confused and lonely and angry at the world. I can say in all honesty, "She's safe with us."

At least, she will be until she decides she wants us to help her jump off the bridge. Guilt chews at my insides like a hungry rat. I stare at my feet as he heads into the kitchen.

Robert's smile has vanished, replaced by a weariness I've never seen on anyone's face before. He pours himself a cup of coffee, takes a drink from it—black—and has a seat at the dining table.

"She's getting worse. She's more susceptible to illness. It's a double-edged sword, really; I know keeping her in the house isn't good for her mental state, but going out so much isn't good for her physically."

I'm not sure why he's telling me all this. He's talking to me like I'm...an adult. Not some punk teenager who's too scared to give a presentation in class or who freaks out sometimes, who has to curl up on his floor and wait for the medicine to kick in before he can function again. In that moment, looking at Robert's tired face—he looks so much like Casper—I think that I really, really don't want to let him down.

"I want to do whatever's best for her," I say.

He rolls his gaze up to me. "How long have you two known each other?"

"A few months. And I know that might seem weird, but we're...we're a lot alike. Me, her, and Adam. I don't know how to explain it, but if there's something I should do to help, tell me."

Robert studies me, thoughtful. "Just take care of her. We've been considering quitting our jobs just to be here. We would have sooner, but we needed the medical benefits for her care. Now that she's..." His voice catches; he swallows back the word *dying*. "Now we need the benefits to make sure we can keep her as comfortable as possible for as long as we can. If you could convince her not to sneak out, you and Adam are welcome to come here any time you want."

An open invite to come and go as we please? I guess that's okay. It'll be weird, being here instead of at my place, but if it helps, then...

I promise Robert I'll do whatever I can, politely decline his offer of coffee, and leave. I'm not sure what to make of the entire conversation. I never know what to do when people actually treat me like an adult. Maybe because I don't feel like one. Harold does it, too, come to think of it. Despite calling me *kiddo*, his explanation of Maggie's will, the way he handled the whole thing, never once made me out to be some sort of defenseless child.

The idea of not being a kid anymore terrifies me.

I am an adult and I have been hurled out of the world of boys and girls into the fray of men and women, and expected to function as a grown-up when I never functioned very well as a kid.

But in this, in dealing with Casper, I know I have to try anyway.

When I get home, the apartment feels smaller and lonely. I put on one of my Queen records, *Innuendo*, to fill the silence and crawl into bed. I feel like I haven't slept in days. But even now, I don't want to sleep. I'm too worried about Casper, worried about Adam. Wondering if Adam will hate me when he's coherent enough to realize what's happened.

I check Suicide Watch, but the site is still down. No news articles. No weird emails. I put in thought to emailing Corey to see if she is willing to talk to me, but I don't. She hasn't called. Hasn't emailed. And I'm not sure I have the energy to deal with that right now. Not when I'm staring at my empty inbox and thinking how someday Casper is going to fall asleep and never wake up, and how Adam almost did the exact same thing.

What was the wish I made back when Maggie died?

That I wanted something to love. Someone to live for. Someone who would miss me.

Now I have it, and I'm going to lose them.

CHAPTER 23

Over the next two weeks, I see very little of my apartment, and get to know Casper's pretty well. Amanda—her mom—and Robert are there a lot of the time, either using what little vacation time they have left or working from home, but they're nice people and it might be the first time I've been around a family who doesn't seem glad when I leave. In fact, I find myself looking forward to their 'family nights.'

Amanda makes dinner and we play a game or watch a movie. Casper usually rolls her eyes at the idea, but there's a softness to her expression, an absence of her usual harshness, that tells me she doesn't mind as much as she says she does.

From: C Harms <enigmaticism@kooncast.com>

To: Vincent H. <herecomesthesun@beemail.com>

Subject: it's kind of funny

I used to hate family nights. I hated having to take time off from my friends or my own TV shows or whatever. It was a waste of time. So now, even if I like it, I pretend I don't, because they'll know why it's changed. I'm dying and I want to see the people who matter as much as possible.

I'm glad you're here for it.

Casper doesn't act like a dying girl around her parents. In fact, she never mentions it. She doesn't say when she's tired or feels unwell. It's pretty obvious by her face and her eyes, but she's trying.

"Halloween is coming up," Robert mentions at

dinner. "Do you have any plans, Vincent?"

Amanda has made Casper's favorite: corned beef and cabbage and mac & cheese. Casper told me as we headed for the kitchen that she wasn't hungry, but she's eating anyway. This is her part of playing *normal.* She doesn't want to hurt her mom's feelings. She doesn't want her parents to see the idea of eating is so revolting she doesn't even want her favorite foods.

"Oh." I think about the question while watching Casper try to choke down another bite. When I nudge her leg beneath the table, she ignores me. "I hadn't really thought about it."

"Well, what do you usually do?" Amanda asks.

I pick at my food, thinking back to many Halloweens ago where Corey talked me into dressing up and going door to door. It was a disaster. Even the thought of how I felt, running into kids from school out on the street without the safety of teachers or parents around...

My stomach is turning.

"Stay at home and pass out candy," I mutter at my plate.

Robert glances at Casper. It's a quick look, but I catch it from the corner of my eye. "You're welcome to do that here this year, if you want. We'll rent you two some movies, get you snacks..."

I see what he's doing: if I stay in, then Casper won't push as hard to go out because she won't want to go alone. I chew and swallow to buy myself some time before having to speak. "Yeah, um. I think that would be fine."

Casper finishes off her corned beef, says she's full, places her dishes in the sink and retreats from the kitchen. I always feel awkward being left behind with her folks, so I scarf down the rest of my meal until the plate is empty, thank them for dinner, and hurry after her.

She's in the bathroom, throwing up everything she just ate.

And I stand in the doorway like an idiot, unsure what to do. I could hold her hair back, except her hair is so short there's nothing *to* hold back. Instead I keep my eyes politely on the wall.

Only when she's dry-heaving do I turn on the sink and fill a cup. She takes it without a word, using her other hand to flush the toilet before she sits back and gulps the water.

"God, I don't know how much longer I can do this."

I swallow back the lump that forms in my throat and sink down beside her, arms looped around my knees, our hips touching. "You okay?"

Casper swallows noisily and leans her head back with a heavy sigh. "Corned beef does not taste good when it's coming back up."

"Thanks for the mental image. Now I'm going to hurl."

"Toilet's right there."

We look at each other and grin.

Casper pats my knee and slowly gets up. "Just so you know, you don't have to come over on Halloween. Don't let my parents bully you into stuff."

I push myself to my feet. "They aren't bullying me. I don't have any plans, and I want to spend it with you. We can dress up."

She splashes cold water on her face, takes another drink, and looks at me in the mirror. "What about Adam?"

My smile fades. "What about Adam?"

"Going to invite him?"

We step out of the bathroom to relocate to Casper's bedroom across the hall.

"He hasn't returned either of our calls or emails. I doubt he wants to spend Halloween with us."

"You never know." She shrugs, collapsing wearily onto her bed. I guess all that getting sick wore her out. "His mom probably grounded him until he's thirty. For all we know, his phone and internet were taken away."

I want to believe it. Except Adam's mom is never home and I can't imagine, even after what he did, Mrs. Rockswell stuck around to make sure he stayed away from his phone and computer. In fact, if she had, it might have made Adam happy just to get some attention from her. It's all the things she *doesn't* do that hurt him so much.

I wonder if he has any idea what happened with Suicide Watch.

My silence makes Casper heave a big sigh.

"All right, all right. No more Adam-talk. Come on; let's see if we can Google the worst horror movies to watch on a Halloween movie-marathon."

I also wonder if Casper realizes this will be her last Halloween.

CHAPTER 24

I've found a new running path from my apartment building to the river's edge, but too many other people use it. Other joggers, cyclists, dog-walkers. So I drive to the bridge and take my old route Halloween morning, having missed the silence, having missed the bridge itself. I jog across it and stop at the halfway mark, breathing in deep. The air is so cold it stings the insides of my lungs, but it's perfect.

I wonder how long it'll be before Casper comes to this exact spot and jumps. Her words have been reverberating in my head—*I don't know how much longer I can do this.* How much is enough for her? The throwing up, the pain, the exhaustion. And when the time comes, is she really going to hold me to my promise?

After the fact, will her parents know I helped? Will they blame me? Can I play dumb and act like I'm as shocked as they're going to be? I really like Robert and Amanda. I don't want them to hate me. Common sense says they wouldn't understand this is really, truly what their daughter wants.

Maybe I should jump with her.

The thought of dying brings Adam to mind. Of what it would be like to leave him behind. I emailed him again this morning. No response. It's been two weeks on the dot. The hospital wouldn't tell me anything when I called, not after Mrs. Rockswell made such a big deal out of them letting me in there to begin with.

For all I know, Adam could have gone home and tried to kill himself again and I would never know.

This sudden thought leaves me nauseous, reeling, and staring all the way down into the abyss below isn't helping. I sink to my knees, gripping the rails, breathing deep. I don't have my medicine with me. No time to freak out.

  Adam is fine.
  Casper is fine — for now.
  I haven't lost them yet, and everything is okay.
  Breathe, Vincent.
  Just.
  Breathe.

  In this part of California, there is no fall or spring. Summer drops right into winter, into summer, back and forth. Our idea of autumn is October, where the leaves rapidly go from green to gold to on-the-ground, and it's suddenly freezing. The van makes a funny noise when I turn the heater on, so I don't bother.
  I arrive home around noon, but it hasn't warmed up much since I set out jogging early this morning. Little clouds form in front of my face when I exhale through my mouth. *Puff puff puff.* Like I'm a train. I probably look like an idiot to anyone watching me. Which is why I stop short near the stairwell leading to my apartment, where Adam is sitting.
  He's hunched forward in a hoodie that was too much in summer, but not enough in winter. His guitar is strapped to his back, hands in his pockets, bike leaning against the railings, and a duffel bag at his feet.
  I stare at him with my breath clouding in front of me and my heart expanding to fill every free inch of my chest cavity. It's beating so hard it hurts.
  Adam notices me even in my silence and lifts his head. He stands quickly, shoving his hood back. His hair is messy, like he just rolled out of bed, and he says with the scratchiness of someone who's been sitting in the cold too long, "Did you mean it?"
  I swallow hard. "Mean what?"

"When you said you would miss me."

God, I could punch his pretty face.

Instead I close the distance between us and hug him tighter than I've ever hugged anyone.

Tighter than I hugged Corey the last time I saw her and was convinced I'd never see her again. Adam puts his arms around me and squeezes back. We're both so cold, but hanging onto each other, we're warm and we're okay. He's okay. I'm okay. He's alive and he's here.

"I miss you right now," I mumble into his neck. Adam tightens his grip. There's a tiny tremor to his hand. He is shivering. It's the only reason I pull away and lead him up the stairs. We drag his bike along and leave it just outside the door.

The heater's been running inside the apartment, so it's toasty. Adam breathes a sigh of relief. I set his bag on the floor and he gingerly removes his guitar, leaning it next to my shelf of records.

"What happened?" I ask.

Adam sniffs. His cheeks and nose are red from the chill. He sits on the edge of the bed. "The hospital kept me for a week for observation to make sure I wasn't 'a threat to myself or others.'"

I kneel at his feet so I can peer up into his face. "Then you went home?"

His mouth twists uncomfortably. Casper is a talker. She can talk a lot, and she can talk honestly. I can talk, but I trip over my words and sometimes say more than I mean to. But Adam...I can physically see the effort it takes for him to open his mouth and force out the words. He's spent so much of his life not being seen, not being heard, that he's forgotten how to realize anything he says does hold weight and is important.

I try to help him along by asking, "Did she kick you out?"

Adam shakes his head. " Sort...of?" He takes a deep

breath. "When we got home, she was so mad. She said I was selfish because she had lost dad and I almost made her lose her son. I told her...she'd lost me a long time ago. She gave me an ultimatum. If I wanted to keep living there, I had to go to therapy. Like, at a rehab center."

"God, you're not on drugs."

He actually cracks a tiny smile. "They have clinics for suicidal people, too."

"Oh."

"I told her I would go to therapy but that I didn't want to live there anymore regardless. I got on my bike and left." The intensity with which he's studying his hands tells me how nervous he is. How embarrassed. "I probably should've made sure I had somewhere to go first."

I want to hug him again.

I inch forward and fold my arms across his knees. I don't want to know how long it took him to ride his bike from his place to mine, because it would probably make me cry. "You already knew. Somewhere in the back of your head, you knew you could come here."

Adam closes his eyes. He bows down until his forehead rests against mine, and his fingers lace together behind my neck. Every spot where our skin is touching, every centimeter where we come together is warmth and understanding and home in a way I've never known it. Because I understand Adam's loneliness just as he understands mine, and he knew, without me ever having to say a word, that he could find sanctuary here.

"Thank you," he murmurs. I wonder if he'd let me kiss him. Because I really, really want to. But what we're doing right now seems more intimate than that, and I don't want to ruin it, so I close my eyes and enjoy the fact that it's no longer cold and we're sharing breath.

Eventually I say, brightly, "We have a Halloween party to get to."

☆

We arrive at Casper's house in full costume. Or, well, as full costume as we could get at the last minute.

Adam's hair is gelled and spiked, and he's sporting black leather fingerless gloves, his hoodie, which has silver studs for decoration on the shoulders, and a pair of mid-calf leather boots that I think are sexy on him but I would never admit to thinking. His guitar is slung across his back for added effect.

He's thinner than I am, but his shirts fit me so I'm in black jeans and one of his well-worn tees with my own black jacket. We did well enough that when Amanda and Robert let us in and we pause in Casper's doorway to say, "Trick-or-treat," she takes one look at us and bursts out laughing.

"Oh my God. What're you supposed to be?"

Adam frowns. "Rockers."

"What, like the Beatles or something?"

My expression deadpans. "No. Nothing at all like the Beatles, actually."

Adam adds, "In our defense, it was really last-minute."

Casper shakes her head. "What about makeup?"

"Why would Adam or I have makeup?"

"Oh, nevermind. Come on."

We follow her to the bathroom where she digs out a makeup box from under the sink. I'd guess with how buried it is, she hasn't used it in awhile. She brandishes an eyeliner pencil, nudges Adam to sit on the lid of the toilet, and gets to work. To Adam's credit, he sits very still. When she's done with him, she turns on me and does the same. "We need to paint your nails. For added effect."

"You're enjoying this too much," Adam mutters, checking out his face in the mirror.

I'm trying not to blink, but it's terrifying. I keep waiting for her to jab me in the eye. "What about you? We need to dress you up."

She pauses, nose crinkling. "Yeah...no. I don't think I own anything that could be considered 'rocker.'"

"Something else, then." I blink rapidly as she draws away, then get up to peek in the mirror. I look like a raccoon.

"Bubblegum Goth," Adam suggests.

"Ha ha. No." Casper stands between me and Adam and all three of us stare in the mirror. She's studying her face. "Let's make me a zombie."

Adam says, "Morbid," and she smacks his arm.

"I'm serious. Vince, go find me some ratty clothes. Adam can do my makeup."

I leave Adam to deal with that while I go into Casper's room and begin rifling through her closet. Finding something for a zombie costume in a wardrobe befitting Rainbow Brite isn't easy. I manage to locate an old pair of jeans with holes in the knees, acid washed and made to look dirty along the thighs. I never got the purpose of buying pants that *looked* stained and ripped, but it must be a girl thing. I find a ratty t-shirt that has to be four sizes too big for her, and has a small tear in the shoulder. Once upon a time it had a decal of a band logo, but it's so cracked and faded I can't make out who it's supposed to be.

When I join them in the bathroom, Casper's face is covered in white, and the dark circles beneath her eyes have been accented with eye-shadow. Adam is in the process of using more shadow to give her mouth a gray tint. I flicker to an image of Maggie in her casket, wax-like, cold. I shiver.

Casper's eyes dart to me. "What'd you find?"

I hold up the shirt and pants. Her gaze lands on the shirt and her mouth downturns, expression going blank, before she nudges Adam away. "I'll finish up and get dressed. I know you're both queer as monkeys, but you're not watching me change."

We're pushed out of the bathroom with little choice but to retreat to her bedroom. Adam goes to rub his eyes, remembers his makeup, and makes a face.

"It looks kind of nice on you," I admit. He gives me a tiny smile.

"It looks nice on you, too."

"Liar."

"I am lying. Sorry." Our eyes meet for half a second before we grin and look away. "You have one of those faces... I don't know. It's sad when anything detracts from your eyes."

That gives me pause. Did he just compliment me? We look at each other again. There's no way he isn't as aware of me as I am of him or of the gap that seems to have been closed between us even in a few short hours.

For half a second, I think I might try to kiss him. Just quickly.

Maybe on the cheek, or the corner of his mouth—

The bathroom door swings open. Casper shuffles across the hall and into the room, arms jutting out in front of her, eyes rolled back, groaning.

"Convincing," I say, heart pounding a beat too fast. Not because of her, but because if she hadn't shown up I honestly would have tried to kiss Adam.

Casper lets her arms drop, gray mouth twisted up into a smile.

"Whose shirt is that?" Adam asks, tugging on her sleeve. One side of it is slipping partway down her thin shoulder. Casper tugs it back up, ruffles her own short hair, and turns away.

"It belonged to Joshua. My boyfriend."

I have the sudden urge to sink into the floor and die. Did I seriously pick out the one shirt in her entire closet that was sure to bring up things she didn't want to think about? "I'm sorry."

"Don't be. It's comfortable. Still smells a little like him." She plops onto her bed and pulls on a pair of clean socks. "Just because we don't talk anymore doesn't mean I shouldn't remember the happy things, right?"

Adam and I exchange looks before I offer, "Why don't you call him?"

"God, no. Last I heard, he was dating someone else. I stopped talking to him for a reason and I'm not going to confuse him by taking it back this close to..." Her words trail off, leaving behind a heavy silence of everything she isn't saying.

This close to the end. Right.

Casper rolls her eyes, like the topic annoys her somehow, and turns away. "I want to hit up a few houses for candy before the street is flooded with brats. Let's go."

She fetches a few plastic bags for candy before we traipse into the kitchen where her parents are filling a big orange bowl with suckers. We say in unison: "Trick-or-Treat!" They both turn to stare at us.

There's a laugh that quickly dies on their lips when they see Casper. Robert recovers quickly enough with a smile that is all too forced, but Amanda's lower lip quivers. Glassy-eyed, she manages a mousy *excuse me* before hurrying out of the room.

Casper's face is stone, like she didn't notice a thing. She shoves her plastic bag out to Robert, hard smile in place. "Do we get candy?"

Robert's jaw is tight with the effort he's putting toward not crying. He scoops up a handful of suckers and deposits them into each of our bags. I'm not sure what the point is. I don't care for candy, and Casper doesn't care for much of anything edible anymore, but she grins and winds her arm around her dad's waist in a quick, firm hug. Robert kisses the top of her head.

"Are you sure about going out...?"

"We're just stopping by a few places. Be back in twenty minutes," Casper assures him, and we leave the house and pretend we don't hear Amanda sobbing in the back room.

☆

It's barely dark outside when we leave, but by the time we reach the end of the block, we have bags half-full of sweets and the street lamps have come on. Casper's steps are slower than I remember them being, and I'm about to suggest we go home when she trips over—something. A crack in the sidewalk, her own feet, I don't know.

Between Adam and me, we barely manage to keep her from face-planting on the pavement, and I panic because her eyes are closed and I think she's unconscious. She sucks in a breath, cursing, trying to regain her bearings, which doesn't seem to be happening.

"Fuck, I need—goddammit." She leans into Adam, abandoning her bag. "I need to sit down."

I rescue her candy and we usher her to a bench at the park across the street. Casper slumps forward, head in her hands like she might be sick. Swearing over and over again beneath her breath.

"We can carry you home," Adam whispers. "Or I can get your dad. Have him drive up here."

"So he'll never let me out of the house again? Right." She hiccups, sniffs, and I realize she's crying. I have never seen her cry before. "I think we got enough candy. Let's go home."

Just like that, our trick-or-treating adventure is over. Casper cries silently the whole way home. I try not to think about how this is the last time she will ever go trick-or-treating, and how she spent it hardly able to walk.

Robert and Amanda retire for the night when we get home, giving us free reign of the kitchen and living room for our horror movies and food. Adam makes some popcorn while I get Casper settled on the pull-out sofa bed—trying to be obscure so her parents don't realize how much she's worn herself out—and retrieve blankets and pillows from her room. I'm not sure her parents considered the idea of us all sleeping out here together, but I decide not to mention it. Lucky me, I get to sleep in the middle.

Together we curl up on the pull-out, staying awake late into the night. Adam is the first one to fall asleep, nestled up against my side with his back to me. We've shared a bed before, always with Casper, sometimes on the floor, but I've never wondered as bad as I'm wondering right now what it would feel like to wrap myself around him and press my face into his hair.

Casper's head rests on my shoulder, her eyes half-lidded. I'm not sure either of us are watching the movie anymore so much as we're fighting sleep.

"Are you still awake?" she whispers. I make a noise to confirm that I am. Casper tilts her chin back, trying to look up at me. "When I'm gone, I want you to give the police all the screen-shots and emails I saved regarding Suicide Watch. Give them my emails from Joey. I want them to know he wasn't ready to die."

I'm too tired to process that fully, which is why I agree so easily with an, "Uh-huh."

"But *I'm* ready."

Any sleepiness I felt vanishes in an instant. My eyes open; alert, awake, I shift to sitting until I can stare down at her. She rests a hand on my arm, signaling me to not speak and risk waking Adam.

"Not right this second. God. Calm down. Just..." She sighs. "This week sometime."

My jaw tightens, teeth clenching, trying to focus so I don't get upset. "Why? You're not... You're still..."

"This is the first day I've gotten out of bed since I saw you last," she says. "I couldn't even take a walk down the street without doping up on pain-killers and falling all over myself. I have to take baths because standing up in the shower is too much effort. My legs are swelling and I'm throwing up every time I try to eat. Even my thoughts are so... I can't...I just...I *hurt*, Vinny. I don't want this anymore."

Her voice is so soft and tired and I know...this is it. This is what the last few months have led up to, and even if I've dreaded it, worried about it, I haven't *prepared* myself for it. Not at all.

Slowly, I lie back down. I slip my arms around her and she comes to me easily, tiny and delicate, and she curls her fingers into my shirt and hides her face against my chest. I don't say anything, because I don't need to.

I made a promise. Now I'm going to have to keep it.

SUICIDE WATCH

Kelley York

November

SUICIDE WATCH

CHAPTER 25

Casper has everything planned out.

Friday night is when she wants to do this. One week after Halloween. She leaves it to me to tell Adam, because—justifiably so—he's upset. He throws a pair of socks across my (our?) apartment and says nothing, but I'm getting good at reading his silences. This isn't a good silence.

"Maybe she'll change her mind," I offer, but Adam looks at me, and we both know it's nothing more than wishful thinking. That night, he finds my hand as I'm drifting off to sleep, and laces our fingers together. When Casper is gone, it will be just the two of us. We're going to need that.

We spend every day that week at Casper's. She's too tired to go out and it's obvious she's not happy about it. Monday and Tuesday, she gets angry over not feeling up to a trip to the movies. By Wednesday, she's quieted down and seems almost resigned. When we show up on Thursday, she's bowed over her desk, scribbling.

"Letters," she tells me. "I don't have everyone's email addresses."

I look at the stack of them. "Do you want me to make sure they're delivered?"

"Yes. But if you don't actually do it, that's okay. I'm not going to be around to care." She crams the letter into an envelope, places it with the others, and puts them in a drawer where her parents won't see.

Adam hasn't talked much.

I think I talk too much. Even though I have no idea what to say.

When we go home at night, neither of us say a word.

Friday, Casper has instructed us not to come over. She wants to spend the day with her parents. One last family night.

Adam and I spend the day absolutely nauseous, unable to eat, unable to think about anything else. I catch him with his guitar on the balcony, plucking at the strings in a tune I instantly recognize as Bob Dylan. He stops when he notices me in the doorway, but his eyes never leave the bridge in the distance. "Are we really going to do this?"

"You don't have to. It was my promise." I step outside, hugging myself against the cold. "I don't want you to think you—"

"I need to be there for her." He tips his head back, peering at me through his mop of dark hair. "After everything she's done for us, we need to be there."

There is no argument for that. I can't even put my finger on what it is Casper's done for us, but she's done something.

And that something is why we pull up outside her house a little after midnight, and Adam sneaks to the front door to help Casper out because she can't do it so well on her own. It was only a few weeks ago that she came darting across the street in the middle of the night with no problems. A few weeks.

Only a few months since she found out about Maggie dying and said *Sorry, that sucks.*

A week since she touched my arm and told me she was ready to die.

Armed with the letters she wrote to her old friends, Casper lets Adam help her into the car. They sit in the back seat, hip to hip, Adam's arm around her weary frame, and I drive to the bridge.

We park in my usual spot. Casper refuses to let us carry her. She wants to walk on her own. Together the three of us, soon to be two, head down the bridge, hoods pulled up, heads down, moving slow so Casper can keep up. It's so cold. The wind is angry tonight, gnawing at our clothes, and more than once the ties on my hood smack me in the face.

Adam brought his guitar at Casper's request. We move to Jessica the Jumper's spot and sit down to shield us from the wind. "What do you want me to play?" he asks.

Casper lifts one shoulder in a shrug. "Something. Anything. Pick something you think I would like."

"Blackbird," I suggest. Adam bows his head, brushes his fingers over the guitar strings, and nods.

It's the first time I've heard him sing. His callused fingertips pluck at the chords and the rest of the world melts away as we listen to the sound of him. He has a beautiful voice. Soft and pained and I want to reach out and gather him up. Gather *both* of them up and promise everything will be okay. I want to protect them. To love them and go far, far away where none of this exists — not the bridge, not Casper's cancer, not Adam's mom. Not anything that breaks us down and brings us to this.

I am helpless.

Adam sings extra verses. To buy time, I think. Waiting for Casper to say *nevermind, let's go home*. She doesn't. Eventually, he stops. There are tears on Casper's face, but she's smiling. "Told you he was good." Simultaneously, she and I reach for each other's hands. I grip her small fingers in mine, and I try to blink back the tears when she says, "Help me up."

We stand. Casper braces herself against the railing and looks out over the water. I think about how this is going to feel. How *much* we're going to feel until we never want to feel again. And I think — we could jump. All three of us.

Together.

There don't need to be any goodbyes.

As though she knows what I'm thinking, Casper squeezes my hand and her eyes meet mine. I know what she wants. What she needs. And my stomach is twisting and turning, but I swing a leg over the railing for the other side, while Adam helps her from his side, because she doesn't have the strength to do it herself.

We're helping our best friend die. She wouldn't be able to do this without us.

I hold onto the railing with one hand and onto Casper with the other. It's dark. Hard to see where the ledge ends and open sky begins. Adam remains where he is. When I look back, his eyes are wide, gold pools of worry and fear, and I realize he thinks I might jump, too.

I could.

But I don't think about jumping with only Casper, because the idea of leaving Adam behind, alone, is too much. It's more frightening than thinking ten minutes, five minutes ahead. Of what tomorrow will bring when Casper is gone.

Her breathing can be heard over the sound of the wind. She leans forward, staring down with tears on her face. She's frightened. It's nothing like Jessica. There is no peace. There is no resolve.

We stay there and the minutes tick by. Three and then four. Five. Casper loosens her grip on my hand, holding onto the rails by herself. It takes everything I have not to reach out and grab her around the waist.

Her eyes fall closed.

And—

"God, I can't..."

There is nothing left to say.

She tries to turn to me, reaching, sobbing, "I'm sorry, I'm sorry." We stumble in my attempt to grab her so quickly. My foot hits a spot I thought would be ledge, but is nothing.

For half a second, I am sure we're both going to fall.

Then Adam lunges forward, his fingers like a vice around my arm.

It's a group effort to get us back over the railing, and we collapse, a mess of tears. A mess of everything.

We are all broken.

CHAPTER 26

Casper is a tiny ball in the back seat, her back to Adam and me. I don't know if she's sleeping, so Adam and I don't talk. Maybe we wouldn't know what to say anyway.

The lights are still out at Casper's place. She's too tired to move on her own, so we have no choice but to help her get inside. She stops long enough to grab a letter she left on the dining table. To her parents. If they'd woken up and seen it...

Halfway down the hall, Amanda emerges from the master bedroom, hand clamping over her mouth to keep from screaming. I guess seeing three shadowy figures in your house at four in the morning would be enough to freak someone out.

"God, Mom, it's *me*," Casper hisses.

Amanda rushes forward, looking torn between fear and fury. "You snuck out? Caitlin Lily Harms, how could you—" Her gaze snaps to us, but before she can let loose, Casper grabs her mom's hands.

"It's totally my fault. I went out for a walk and was too tired to come back home. Vinny and Adam drove all the way over here to pick me up. I'm sorry."

Her lie seems to placate Amanda, at least a little; her expression softens as her eyes begin to tear over. She pulls Casper into a tight hug, whimpering against her hair. Casper allows it, squirming away only after a moment or two.

"Let me say goodnight to these two and I'll go back to bed."

Amanda nods, only reluctantly letting go. We help Casper to her room and pull off her coat, her shoes, her socks. She doesn't seem to care about anything beyond that.

"I owe both of you an apology," she says, lying down. "Making you go through that... I don't know what I was thinking. It wasn't fair."

Adam and I stare at the floor.

"I love you both. You know that, right?" Her voice is choked, and it gets us to look up. "I chased away pretty much everyone else I cared about, and by some miracle, I was still able to find you. And by an even bigger miracle, you two have put up with my bullshit." She grins fleetingly. "I just...really love you."

We crawl onto the bed with her, gathering her up into our arms, hugging her, and reassuring her that, yes, we love her, too.

When we leave, Casper gives us a wink and a small wave.

"Behave. Don't do anything I would do."

Home at six a.m. never looked so good. I barely get out of my shoes before I collapse into bed, breathing deep into a pillow. I'm already almost asleep when I realize Adam is still up. Of course he is. He's getting undressed, getting into sleep-clothes and putting his dirty clothes in the laundry. Neat and tidy.

He catches me watching him and blushes, turning away. "What?"

"I like watching you." Oh. I must be way too tired. I shouldn't talk.

A hint of a smile plays across his face, though, as he flicks off the lights, and sinks onto the bed beside me with his guitar. I've heard him playing a handful of times, but until tonight, he's never let me hear him sing. I shift to make more room for him while he gets settled, hoping maybe I'll get to hear it again, without the sound of wind and water drowning out his voice.

Adam strums the chords once, nods to himself, and begins to play.

At first, my chest tightens. *In My Life*—these are the lyrics Adam emailed to Casper and me when he OD'd. It used to be one of my favorites, but I haven't been able to listen to it without feeling overwhelmingly anxious since that night.

Now Adam is playing it, singing it, the tension slowly but surely begins to ebb. It's just us, sitting in the darkness while the moon gives me just enough light to see the outline of him, the shape of his mouth as it moves and the careful, sure way his fingertips glide over the strings. The song is right. '*All these places have their moments.*' Like right now. Right here. Me and him.

For the first time since Adam showed up at my doorstep, things are *okay*, at least for the time being.

We aren't afraid of when we'll watch Casper jump.

We aren't afraid that I would go with her.

Adam knows. I didn't have to say it, but I think he knows that where I want to be, right now, in this moment, is here with him. Even after he's set his guitar aside and has lain down beside me, he murmurs the lyrics against my ear, and soothes me to sleep.

At noon, around the time we crawl out of bed, I have the oddest urge to take Adam to the animal shelter. I haven't been in a week, which is some kind of record for me.

"The animal shelter?" he asks. "Do you want a pet?"

"No. I just...go sometimes. To hang out."

Adam tips his head. "Why?"

"It's relaxing, I guess." Pause. "So, do you want to go?"

He looks pleased. I'm not sure if it's because he's been lonely without animals since he came home from the hospital and found his mom got rid of Crispy the cat, or if he's happy for a change of scenery.

SUICIDE WATCH

Thirty minutes later, we're stepping into the shelter. There are butterflies in my stomach. This place has been my sanctuary for years and I'm not sure what to do having someone with me.

Adam likes cats. We wander the cat rooms, peering through the glass. He smiles as they play, and I suppose it's worth it to not be able to pet them if Adam keeps smiling like that. Especially when he says, "The sign says there are more back here; come on," and grabs my hand.

He doesn't let go.

Neither do I.

We do our rounds with the cats, and finally come full-circle and start in on the other side. The kennels.

"The dogs are more depressing," he observes. I'm instantly scanning the fences for any sign of the dogs I've visited before, only vaguely aware I'm squeezing the hell out of Adam's hand. We don't stop long at any one kennel, because I'm not sure I'm ready for Adam to think what a weirdo I am for what I do when I come here. He has a quiet smile on his face, wanting to pet every dog he comes across whether they're doomed for death or not. He is an equal-opportunity petter.

A few small yappy-type dogs have gotten his attention when he says, "You should get a job here."

"Why would I do that? I don't need the money." Not for a few more months, anyway. Then...well.

Then.

Yeah.

"Something to do." He shrugs, scratching under one of the dog's chin. "Something that isn't sitting around the apartment all day. Being self-sufficient?"

"Because I'm totally fit to be around people all day." I walk off down the aisle, hoping he'll take the hint and drop the subject. He trails after me.

At the end of the row, in the back corner of the massive room, is a roped-off area of kennels. New arrivals that are quarantined while being tested for diseases and temperament. A few big mutts snarl and bark in my direction. I doubt there's much hope for them. Stupid. So stupid. They're just scared, so they lash out. They're no different than the dog in the far back kennel, huddling and shaking. We all deal with fear differently.

The barking dogs are like Casper. Angry and trying to play tough because they think it'll keep them safe, not realizing that in the end, they're only hurting themselves by pushing everyone away. Then there are the dogs that lay in the back of their kennels, heads down, avoiding eye contact. They are Adam. Keeping their gazes lowered and never confronting anything.

Then there is the dog in the corner, trembling. Before I realize what I'm doing, I'm lifting the rope, ducking beneath, and making my way over to stand in front of its kennel. The tag on his fence says he was brought in yesterday. No name. Guesstimated age: two years.

I look down at him. He looks up at me, tongue lolling out of his mouth as he pants, and his tail thumps feebly against the floor. I press my hand to the chain link and the nameless dog ducks his head, watching me warily, before picking himself up to walk over to me.

Adam lingers close at my side. I hadn't realized he'd followed. "He's kind of a hot mess."

He is. His back right leg is twisted a bit funny. One of his ears is half-missing, lined with stitches where something—metal or the bite of another dog—took a chunk out of it. It's red and swollen like it might be infected. Add that to his weird, marbled coloring, mismatched eyes and the crooked way he walks, he is kind of a mess.

I sink down. The dog sniffs at my fingers. He could bite me. I could get rabies and die. There's a reason this area is closed off to the public. But the dog whimpers quietly then licks me. Adam crouches. The dog's tail wags so hard I think he's going to throw himself off-balance and fall.

Adam slips his fingers through the gate. We're going to get caught, but neither of us seems to care. Dog whines and rolls his eyes — one blue, one brown — to Adam's face and slobbers all over his hand.

I am in love.

"See," Adam whispers, "It isn't about the people, you know? It's about the animals. You could do something that involves taking care of them rather than dealing with customers. Like—"

"I don't want a *job*, Adam," I snap, and instantly regret it with the wounded look he gives me. Even the dog recoils, backing away like I've just crippled its other leg. My chest constricts. I turn away and duck back under the rope, hurry out of the kennels, out of the shelter, retreating. Cowering, because I'm so good at that.

What does he expect? That I can get a job, function normally, and live a normal life until I'm ready to die? Not that I've made up my mind either way, because what I do largely depends on too many factors I can't even begin to predict—

(Casper.)

(Adam.)

(My own moods.)

—but the idea of getting settled into anything that involves daily interaction with strangers is terrifying.

When Adam finds me I'm in the van, staring at my hands in my lap. Embarrassed for getting so upset and running out like I did. Embarrassed that I'm still trying to get a grip on my emotions. Humiliated because there's no legitimate reason for me to be on the verge of tears like a fucking five-year-old without knowing how to even express what's wrong with me.

What *is* wrong with me?

He says nothing. Only buckles himself in and we sit there for awhile in silence while I try to calm down.

Just when I think he might say something, his phone

pings. The noise I've come to recognize as an email rather than a text or a call. Not that anyone ever calls him. He takes a breath, holds it a few seconds, then fishes his phone out of his pocket.

I don't think anything of it. Not until Adam's choked, feeble voice snaps me out of my daze.

"We need to go."

SUICIDE WATCH

CHAPTER 27

There are three cars outside Casper's house I don't recognize. I pound on the front door with more effort than is necessary until an unfamiliar older woman pulls it open and frowns at us.

"Can I help you?"

We only ran across the street, but I'm out of breath from adrenaline squeezing my lungs tight. "Is Casper home?"

"Sorry?"

"Caitlin," Adam corrects quickly. "We're here to see Caitlin."

The woman's mouth tightens. I think she's about to tell us to get lost when Robert appears over her shoulder. "It's all right, Diane. They can come in."

Diane smiles thinly. She steps aside and disappears into the living room, where other strangers are seated. I don't see Amanda. More importantly, I don't see Casper.

I can't stop shaking.

Robert doesn't look so hot. His eyes are red and shadowed, his hair a mess, his beard in need of a trim. He takes a seat at the table and we sit across from him. My mind has an almost wooly, thick feel to it, and I can't find words. For once, Adam succeeds where I fail.

"What's going on...?"

Casper's dad runs his hands over his face, taking a few deep breaths. "Boys. Caitlin passed away this morning."

No. No, no, no.

That isn't.

It's not.

"We just..."

I can't breathe.

"...saw her. Last night. She was..."

My voice cracks. Adam grabs my hand.

"We think she might have overdosed on her morphine pills," Robert whispers. "Whether it was on purpose or not..."

If I weren't already sitting, I would have hit the floor by now.

Where is that all-encompassing numbness I felt when Maggie died? I want it back. I want to feel nothing because this hurts too much and seeing Robert's miserable, heartbroken face is going to kill me.

"You boys. You two were..." He's crying now, every word a struggle to keep steady, to force out. "You made her so happy. She had friends who were there for her as much as you were and I'm...so very, very grateful. I can't even begin to..."

He presses a hand over his face.

Robert excuses himself and vanishes into the back room. One of the ladies from the living room, who I think must be an aunt of Casper's, explains Amanda is lying down and Robert might not be the best for company right now. She's very kind, but it's clear we are not family and thus aren't welcome in the house at this exact moment in time.

We climb into the van. We drive home. Scale the stairs. We sit side-by-side on the bed, holding hands. I can feel Adam's pulse through his thumb pressed against my knuckle.

Breathe in. Breathe out. We are alive. And she's gone.

It hurts.

I sleep with my face pressed into Adam's neck, where my tears have dried. Our legs are tangled together. Hands clasped tightly.

Breathe in, breathe out. Over and over again.

Just to prove a broken heart can't really kill you.

CHAPTER 28

From: C Harms <enigmaticism@kooncast.com>

To: Vincent H. <herecomesthesun@beemail.com>;

Adam Roxy <adayinthelife@beemail.com>

Subject: Darling Boys

I think the bridge was this grand thought in my head because I wanted to go out with a bang, you know? Fly off into oblivion or whatever. I can't say I'm sorry enough for putting you both through that. I almost made a huge mistake.

But I meant it, you know? When I said I was ready to go.

It was the method I chose that was all wrong.

I hate that my parents will find me.

I hate that you'll be angry with me.

Maybe not at first, but you will. Eventually. It's all part of the process, isn't it?

I didn't leave them that letter. I realized they aren't going to get the money from my life-insurance policy if it comes out I killed myself, and God knows they're going to need the fundage for all the medical bills I've racked up.

But this whole situation is pretty FUBAR without any real fix that will make everyone happy. I guess that's life. And death. And everything in-between.

I also meant it when I said I loved you both. You made the last few months of my life beautiful, and maybe a part of me wants to die with the thought I was able to do something amazing like bringing two people together. I wish I had cornered you guys and found out for sure if I'd succeeded in that. If I did, well, there's my legacy. Pretty fucking awesome.

Vinny, take a look at the blog I forwarded you. Thought you might find it interesting.

Keep fighting.

You have the rest of your lives to fix what's broken.

And the "rest of your life" is only as short as you make it.

Goodbye.

All my love,

C.

CHAPTER 29

The world is dimmer.
Adam is restless.
I am numb.
I wish he would cry. Or get angry. Or something. But he just paces the apartment. Showers twice a day. Sometimes he gets on his bike and goes for a ride. Which is okay because he doesn't go with me on my morning jogs.
We need our alone time, I think.
At night Adam curls around me and we hold each other, and I really want to kiss him and promise everything will be okay. It would be an empty promise, though, and I won't make a promise I can't keep. We're like this unspoken couple who is too crippled and heartbroken to begin to know how to function or provide comfort.
The posting Casper forwarded me is a blog entry from a local woman whose sister went missing. It's from last January. They had an argument, it says. Two weeks later they found the girl's body in the river.
Her name was Jessica Mallory.
My jumper.
Jessica died thinking no one would miss her. Not a week goes by on this blog without an entry talking about Jessica. She is missed. Her family still mourns, still regrets.
A mystery is solved.
I buy a newspaper to cut out Casper's obituary. I have no idea what to do with it. It's just a flimsy piece of gray paper with ink that is getting on my fingers. Casper's face is a smiling one. An old photo from her chubbier days where she looked so bright and happy and healthy. Better days.

SUICIDE WATCH

Roger and Amanda give us all the information for Casper's funeral, but we debate the entire night before on whether or not we should go. We won't know anyone. No one will know us. I could medicate myself beforehand, make it so I don't care what anyone else might think or say, yet doing it — numbing myself for her funeral — seems so disrespectful and cruel.

In the end, we do go. We dress nicely (wouldn't Maggie be proud?) and show up to the chapel where a ton of people have already assembled. Old people, people from her family, people from her school. Adam must sense my discomfort when we walk in and a few heads turn, because he takes my hand and doesn't let go.

We head to the front long enough to give Amanda and Robert our condolences. *I'm sorry for your loss*, because we are, and I thought people saying that sort of thing to me at Maggie's funeral was stupid, but it seems to make Casper's parents feel better. That's all that matters. Then we retreat to the back of the room and stay put. Listening. Here for support, because we loved her, but funerals are so much more for the family than the deceased, aren't they?

(Everyone is here to tell her goodbye. My question still stands: How do you say goodbye to someone who is already gone?)

Amanda seeks us out again before we can leave, and gives us both a big hug. "Don't be strangers," she says. "You're welcome to drop by. Anytime you want. Got it?"

As we head for the doors, I spot a couple guys and girls close to our age milling about near the front of the room. I vaguely recognize their faces from the photo in Casper's room. Her friends. Her ex-boyfriend. The ones she pushed aside. Obviously, she didn't push hard enough because here they are.

So many people loved Caitlin Harms. I wish I could tell her *that* is her legacy.

"The letters," Adam whispers.

Yes. The letters. Part of the reason we ultimately decided to show up. I had no idea if Caitlin's old friends would be here, but for some reason I really wanted to hand-deliver these rather than drop them in the mail.

I slide them from my coat pocket and we approach the group. They quiet down and turn to us, sad but curious. The only one whose name I know — "Are you Joshua?"

The tall boy straightens up. "Yeah. Who're you?"

"We were friends of Caitlin's," Adam says. He nudges me.

"These are from her. We promised we'd deliver them." I hold out the handful of letters, with Joshua's at the top of the stack.

An indescribable sadness passes over Joshua's face as he takes the envelopes from my hand. He says "Thanks" like an automatic reaction. Good manners engrained that don't fail him even now.

Neither Adam nor I know what else to say, so we nod, turn, and leave. I'm curious to know what the letters say. What Casper's last words would've been to a guy she obviously cared about so much.

The drive home is a long one. Maybe because the van barely sputtered to life, and I'm listening closely for any other weird sounds. I guess I should have it looked at. At the apartment, I head upstairs and Adam gestures for me to go on up while he checks a voicemail he got while we were at the service. I've just gotten out of my button-up shirt when Adam finally joins me.

"Don't kill me, but I have somewhere I need to go. You okay for a bit?"

I'm still yanking at my tie to get it undone, frowning. "What?"

Anxious knots twist up in my abdomen. Where is he going? Why? Right after a *funeral*? I follow him onto the porch, shirt still in hand, tie dangling around my neck half-undone, almost pathetically frantic because something unplanned is happening and I don't know what's going on. "Adam—"

He unlocks his bike from the railing, stops, turns to me. "I'll bring dinner back, okay?" Before I can get another word out, Adam silences me with a quick kiss. Right on my mouth.

I can't move.

Adam carries his bike down the stairs, swings onto the seat, and takes off.

What the hell just happened?

I should be upset he ran off on me like that. Then again, he *did* kiss me, and that sort of makes up for pretty much anything.

One of my neighbors emerges from the apartment next door. There's a hitch in his step when our eyes meet, and the odd look he gives reminds me I'm standing outside half-dressed, and God knows what kind of stupid expression I have on my face. I duck inside, cheeks warm, and get changed.

Something significant just happened. He *kissed me*.

I almost go for my computer to email Casper. The reality that she won't answer drags me out of my momentary bliss, and I am left staring at the laptop on my bed, feeling idiotic for even having thought it. It's just me and Adam now.

Being alone in the apartment is too much. I want to think about Adam kissing me because it's happier, and then I feel guilty for wanting to be happy after attending the funeral of one of my only friends.

After I get changed into something more comfortable, I hop in the van to go...somewhere. I don't know. The van turns over reluctantly, but it starts. As long as it starts, we're good, right? The heat already doesn't work. Neither does the A/C. I end up a few blocks away at the store, long enough to grab some milk and chips. We always need milk and chips.

As soon as I try to start the van to head home, it sputters, whines, and dies. I try again. This time...nothing. Dead. I don't know whether to laugh or cry. My emotions are wired all wrong anyway, so who the hell knows what kind of reaction this situation will trigger?

In the end, I laugh. I hit my palms against my thighs, rest my head on the steering wheel, and *laugh*, because this really fucking figures.

These are the times I wish I'd had some kind of normal upbringing. A normal set of parents who would teach me what to do when situations like this came up. Maggie was a great foster-mom, don't get me wrong, but she never thought to teach me all the little stuff. How to pay bills or balance a checkbook, how to register a car, what to do to get my damned internet activated.

Or what to do when my car breaks down.

I can't just leave it here, can I? What will Adam say when he comes home and finds me gone? Logically, I am only dimly aware this is not the end of the world but I keep thinking *Casper would know what to do.* My mind is a frazzled mess of thoughts and panic and I am suddenly so very glad I never deleted Harold's number from my phone like I said I would.

"*Hello? Vincent?*"

"The van broke down and I'm stuck at the store and I have no idea what to do," I say in a rush, feeling instantly guilty and humiliated I would call him with such a thing. I'm eighteen years old. I'm an *adult* and I can't even figure out what to do with something as simple as this?

Harold takes a deep breath. "*Okay. What's it doing?*"

I let out another short half-sob, half-laugh. "It's not starting, is what it's doing. I'm turning the key and it's not...doing...anything."

"*Okay, okay. Calm down, kiddo. Tell me where you're at and I'll be right there.*"

Harold writes down the address and I hang up, staring at my phone. Wondering how crazy Harold thinks I am right now. I'm such a brat.

Thirty minutes later, Harold pulls up in his black sedan, bringing with him a small duffel bag. He must've been at the office or something, because he's still in his work clothes, sans blazer, and he's unbuttoning his cuffs to roll up his sleeves. I get out of the van, toeing at the ground and avoiding his gaze, but he smiles.

"Harold's car service to the rescue. Want to pop the hood for me?"

I stare at him blankly for half a second before I recall seeing some sort of button or something inside the van for the hood. Down by the trunk release, right? Thankfully, I don't look like too much of an idiot because I find it quickly enough. Harold props up the hood, flings his tie over his shoulder, opens his duffel bag, and gets to work. I linger nearby, trying to watch what he does, curious but afraid to ask questions.

"You should really think about trading this old thing in," Harold says, a weird device in his hands. "Maggie was stubborn about things like that; she hated buying cars. But no kid like you should be driving around in something nearly twenty years old."

Is the van really that ancient? Geez. My shoulders lift and fall in a quick shrug, and my curiosity gets the better of me. "What's that thing do?"

He's distracted for a second, doing whatever it is he's doing, before he pulls back and straightens his tie. "It's a multimeter. Checks the charge in the battery...which is dead, by the way."

Dead battery. Makes the van sound like a flashlight. "Oh."

"There's an auto parts store up the street. We can swing up there, grab a new one and I can put it in. Save you the pain of taking it to a mechanic." He gives me a smile. I wonder if it's to reassure me or because he's happy I asked him for help. As much as I don't want to accept kindness from Harold, I have to admit, I'd rather deal with this now and get it over with than have to wrangle with mechanics on my own.

Harold takes out the old battery and brings it with us. His car isn't brand new, but it has a brand-new car smell. Something I only know from a few trips in the SUV Corey's parents bought my last month in Southern California. It had twenty miles on it when they drove it off the lot, and smelled like...well, Harold's car. He must spend hours keeping it clean. I guess if he doesn't have a wife anymore, he has that spare time.

I glance at his hand. Nope. Still missing a ring.

"What happened to your wife?"

Harold's expression goes a little weird. It's subtle. Just a squint to his eyes, a vague downturn of his mouth. I quickly look out the window.

"Nevermind. Sorry. None of my business."

He clears his throat, seeming to recover from the shock that I asked him something so personal. "We split up. She, ah, left. About three weeks after Maggie passed away."

"What a shitty time to ditch someone."

Harold bites back a laugh. "We'd been having issues long before that. It just...came to a head."

"Oh." Long pause. I'm not sure if I should keep talking, or let the subject go. It really isn't any of my business, but Harold asks about my well-being all the time, so... "Why?"

The smile on his face is a sad one. "She was seeing someone else. An insurance salesman, if you can believe it."

"She has a thing for guys in hated professions."

"Yeah. I guess she does." Harold chuckles, turning into another parking lot. "It's all right, though. Can't say I blame her. She thought I worked too much, and...well. Why are you asking me all this?"

"I don't know. I guess I'm curious." Maybe I got used to Robert, who talked to me like an adult. Told me things. Like I was one of the guys. I liked that feeling.

Harold nods. He parks in a shaded spot outside the auto store and kills the engine with a deep sigh. I'm about to get out of the car when he speaks back up. "Susan wanted kids. We tried. For several years, in fact. She got pregnant a couple times, but we lost them all."

They...?

Oh.

I stare at him.

"Three miscarriages. Eventually we kind of gave up because she was getting up there in age anyway."

"But if it wasn't your fault," I say slowly, "why was she blaming you?"

"Sometimes people need someone to blame." He shrugs. "Or maybe she didn't *blame me* so much as she was reminded of what we would never have when she looked at me. She met this other guy a few years younger, better looking, who had the time to go out and do things..."

I'm trying to wrap my head around this. "How doesn't that make you really sad?"

Harold twists in his seat toward me. "It does make me sad, Vincent. It makes me really sad."

"You don't look it."

"Just because someone doesn't act or look unhappy doesn't mean their lives are perfect." He raises his eyebrows. "There's this method of dealing with things that involves keeping your chin up. Knowing whatever crap you're dealing with *right now* isn't going to last forever. All things pass."

I was with him up until this point. Because he's wrong. "Not all things." I shove open the door and get out. Harold follows. Not that I'm going anywhere, I'm just...walking a tight circle in the empty parking spot beside his car. "Sometimes bad stuff *does* last. Sometimes it kills you."

Harold puts his hands on his hips. "Will you take a deep breath and talk to me, Vince?"

I stop pacing and look at him. Really, really look at him. Closer than I've ever cared to look at him before. I see he has circles under his eyes from not sleeping. There's a wrinkle in his shirt. His hair isn't combed as neatly as it was last time I saw him. And I realize...he's been smiling at me these last few months, but it was only for my sake. Because he thought I needed him to.

I am the world's shittiest person.

My jaw clenches so tightly it hurts. "I went to a friend's funeral today. She killed herself because she was dying of cancer."

Harold opens his mouth into a startled 'o,' and then his eyes soften. "I'm sorry to hear that, kiddo."

But I'm not done. Suddenly, out of nowhere, my mouth is opening and I'm launching into the details about Suicide Watch. About how Harbinger is in big trouble and I think the evidence I have from my computer and Casper's could get him in even bigger trouble, but the whole thing is *too big* for me to wrap my mind around. I don't know where to start. Who to contact. If I could get in any trouble for it. If Casper's parents would miss out on the life insurance money if it came to light Casper was a part of all this and committed suicide.

Harold listens silently, nodding once in awhile to show he's paying attention. When I'm done, I wipe at my eyes. Not crying, exactly, but close enough that I feel pretty pathetic. How many people have wandered by and stared at the weird kid in the parking lot, going on a rant to the tired lawyer? Sounds like the beginning of a bad joke.

He runs a hand over his face. "You've had a lot going on, haven't you?"

I shrug helplessly, because this isn't really about me. I don't think. It's about Casper and Adam, and Harbinger going to jail so he'll never hurt anyone again.

"Look." Harold's hands come to rest on my shoulders. I force my eyes to meet his. "I told you before, whatever happens, I'm here to help. All right? This whole thing will get taken care of. I'll do some research into the case. You just gather up the evidence, as much as you can, and let me handle the rest."

My shoulders slump, the tension sucked right out of them. "Okay," I say quietly, and then, "Thank you."

The grin he gives me is a comforting one. I know he's troubled by all of this; I can see it in his eyes. He doesn't ask me why I joined the website or why I was talking with Harbinger. He doesn't ask how seriously I was considering killing myself, or if I still am. I don't know if I'd have answers to anything he could possibly ask.

Harold gives my back a pat the way I think a father would. "Let's go get that battery."

The van starts up with only minimal resistance. Harold lets the hood fall shut and circles around to the open driver's side door where I'm half-on the seat and staring at the dashboard like I'm expecting the engine to explode.

"Easy as pie," Harold says, cleaning his hands on some wet-wipes he got at the auto store. "Should be good now. If it starts having problems turning over, let me know and we'll get it into a mechanic. Might be the alternator."

I have no idea what an alternator is or does. Some guy I am. I can name every Top 100 band from the 1960s and tell someone how to beat the final boss of almost every RPG that came out within the last three years, but I never knew before today how to change a car battery.

"I meant what I said, though, about trading this junker in." Harold gives the van a once-over and tugs down his sleeves.

I nod. It's been three hours. Thankfully, it's freezing outside so the milk I bought hasn't gotten warm. "I should...um. Probably get home. My roommate is waiting." Roommate? Is that what I call him? I have no idea. Seems better than explaining where Adam fits into everything.

Harold looks intrigued. "I didn't know you had a roommate."

"It's recent." I duck my head. "He was a friend of Casper's. He wasn't getting along with his mom, so he's been staying with me."

Surprisingly, Harold smiles. "That's great."

"Is it?"

"Sure. I don't like the idea of you being by yourself so much. It's not good for you. Or anyone."

I draw my legs into the car to sit properly. Harold shuts the door and I roll down the window, frowning. "Thanks. Again. I'm sorry I interrupted your day."

"Don't worry about it, kiddo. See you around." He steps back from the van and lifts his hand in a wave. I think about what life is like for him now. If he works longer hours because he misses his wife. If he sits at work and stares at his desk, wondering what it would be like to have pictures of his kids in shiny frames to show off to his clients.

I lean out the window. "Harold."

He stops, turns. "Hm?"

"I think you would've made a great dad."

The apartment is still empty when I get home. I put away the milk and chips, and plop down in front of the television to button-mash through a game. Adam doesn't walk through the door for another hour, but, as promised, he's carting along a bag of food from a Chinese place around the block.

He smiles, breathless from his bike ride, and I almost

forget I'm annoyed with him. And confused. Definitely more confused than annoyed. Like, if I were to get up and kiss the hell out of him, would it be appropriate now?

"It's still hot." He places the bag on the floor and sits beside me. I should probably invest in a dining table at some point. Not that there's a lot of room for one, but I could manage something small, pushed into the corner by the kitchen.

I pause my game mid-zombie slaughter session, hungry enough to grab a pair of chopsticks and dig in without questioning him. He looks *happy*. His hair is brushed back from his eyes, and he does more eating than picking at his food like he normally does. We went to Casper's funeral today. You'd think he'd be less...I don't know.

When he's polished off the last piece of sweet-and-sour chicken: "I got a job."

I almost choke on my chow mein. "What?"

"A job." He swipes at his hair out of habit, used to it being in his face. "At the record shop. The one you told me about?"

The same one I got my records and turntable from, yeah. It's a couple miles away. A long walk, but I guess not too bad biking it. Still—"You got a... *Why?*"

Adam's brows knit together. Obviously, this isn't the reaction he'd expected. (What *did* he expect?) "Money."

"Why would you need money? I—"

"—Have been taking care of me, yeah. I don't like that. It isn't fair to you. How much longer is Maggie's money going to last, Vince?"

It's my turn to frown. I've sort of been avoiding looking at my bank account because there is significantly less in there than I want there to be. I could've stretched it out to a year if I'd watched my savings, but I've been buying stuff pretty freely. Paying for food and gas and movies for Casper and Adam. I'll be lucky if that money gets me through March.

Adam shakes his head and sets his empty box and chopsticks aside. "I appreciate it. I really, really do. Which is why I wanted to help out, you know? I don't have my mom around to tell me what my plans are for college or whatever, so I need to start thinking ahead on my own."

Does he realize what he's saying and what it really, honestly means? Thinking ahead means he's not planning on overdosing again. No jumping. No anything. In terms of Adam, it's a beautiful thing, because I couldn't handle losing him, too.

But when it pertains to me — the idea of looking that far ahead to college and careers and anything beyond *tomorrow* is so big and vast and frightening.

"That's good. That's...you know. Great." I pick myself up off the floor and make for the bathroom. For my medicine. He doesn't need to see my panic-attack.

"Vince?" Adam follows. He sighs when he sees the pill bottle, and plucks it out of my hands before I have a chance to get the lid off.

"Hey!"

"Stop it. Talk to me before you go doping yourself up."

"I'm not—" My eyes are tearing over. I'm so, so tired of crying at everything I shouldn't cry at. Any Man-Card I've ever had has surely been revoked these last few months. "What do you want me to say?"

"Whatever you're thinking. That would be good." Adam perches himself on the bathroom counter, bottle in hand, and studies my distressed face in that intense way of his. Like I'm a knot to be carefully untangled.

"What does it matter, Adam? What does any of it matter?" I wipe roughly at my eyes. "You got a job. That's great. I *mean* that. But what does that mean for *me*?"

It means he's getting better. It means he's *trying*, he's moving forward. It means he is a step away from me because he doesn't need me to take care of him anymore. And I am stuck in place with no clue what to do with myself.

Adam swings his legs a little, looking around the bathroom as though he'll find answers in the sink or the grout between the shower tiles. "No idea. What should it mean? It means you could find a job. Work part-time, if you wanted, and go to college."

"A job doing *what*? Watching animals die?" I'm acutely aware my voice is rising. I don't want to yell at Adam. I really, really don't. "I'm going to spend the rest of my life failing to save dogs and people because what else can I do? I'm fucking useless. I'm stupid and I don't *function* right in the head and people give me panic-attacks and I don't—I can't—It's all too *big*, Adam."

"What is?"

"The future. Everything!"

Adam tosses the bottle of pills aside. It hits the floor and rolls into a corner. He slides off the counter and my back is now against the wall, the corner of a towel rack digging between my shoulder blades. I do not complain because Adam has my face in his hands and he's kissing me and my entire mind turns to mush and it might as well be leaking out my ears.

His mouth is clumsy against mine so I think he hasn't done this much before. I'm no expert, either, so it's almost endearing the way we fumble for some sort of rhythm, but only end up frantically crushing our lips together like we can't stand to be apart. It's terrifying because Adam has all this potential to be something so fucking *amazing* and I would be—

I could be—

I am nothing.

He draws back, breathless. "You're not nothing. You're something to *me*, and you're so much stronger than you think you are. Whatever's broken with either of us…we can *fix* it."

    Jobs. Therapy. More medication? I don't know if I can do it.

SUICIDE WATCH

CHAPTER 30

"How does Adam like his job?" Harold asks when I stop by to drop off the emails a few weeks later. He flips through them, scanning pages, then stacks them neatly at the corner of his desk. I'm glad he's not going over them in detail while I'm standing in his office.

It took a lot for me to let Harold have them at all. Some of those emails contain so many personal thoughts and feelings and when he's done reading, he will know the inner workings of my brain better than most people ever have or ever will. I didn't give him Casper's. Harbinger will certainly be going to jail already with the evidence against him, so the added hassle her parents would have to endure isn't worth it. He only has mine, and I hope it's at all useful somehow.

I shrug in response to his question. "He enjoys it. He spends his day talking music with customers and gets a great discount." In the two weeks he's been there, his—our?—record collection has expanded to twice its original size. Every day he comes home with some sort of present for me, a goofy smile on his face.

The job is good for him. I've never seen him smile so much.

Also have to admit...I'm not doing well being left home alone so much.

"Good." Harold tips his head, studying me. "And how about you?"

"I'm..." Honesty, right? "I've been worse."

He nods once and, almost like an afterthought, he pulls out a business card from his desk drawer. "Here. Take this."

I do. The name on the card in professional, green print is *Amelia Dumar, Psy.D.*. I glance up at Harold. "What is it?"

"My cousin." He leans back in his expensive leather chair, fingers laced together. "She's a psychologist. I was talking to her a little about your situation—" before I can flip out, he adds, "—no details, I promise, and she said to contact her. You and Adam both."

I look at the card. Maybe I have money for bills and we're okay for now, but paying out-of-pocket for a shrink?

"Pro-bono, she said." Harold studies me, like he knows precisely what I'm thinking. "Give her a call if you want. She'll be expecting you."

Nodding, I wrap my hand around the business card. I could cram it in my front pocket because the front pockets are for things I get rid of later. Receipts. Gum wrappers. Maybe I *should* trash it. Last time I saw a shrink, he put me on medication and I never saw him again. Adam says he doesn't think that's what either of us needs.

I thank Harold and I tuck the card into my back pocket, behind my wallet. Safe and sound.

Now that kitten-season has ended, the shelter is quieter than usual. In a few weeks, business will pick back up for Christmas. Families looking for a new pet. The sad statistics are that a large percentage of those cats and dogs will end up right back here, but there are still a few of them who will live out their lives with their new families. Some will be saved. Not all, but some. It's better than none.

The dog with the crippled leg Adam and I saw last time we were here is still in the quarantined section. I glance around to make sure no one is watching, and then duck under the rope. The dog lifts his head and eyes me warily. I wonder if he remembers me snapping at Adam last time. My stomach knots up.

"Hey," I whisper. Dog ducks his head with an

appraising stare, then slowly rises to his feet and hobbles over. Up close, now that I'm paying more attention, it looks as though the bone in his leg is deformed, twisted at an odd angle like it didn't know which way to grow. I push my fingers into the kennel for him to lick, and I scratch under his chin. His good ear flops over and his half-missing one sticks straight up. The stitches are still there, but the painful redness is gone. It's starting to heal.

"You really are kind of a mess, aren't you?"

(You and me both, dog.)

He flops onto his side and rolls over to show me his belly. It makes me smile.

"Hey! You can't be over there!"

I jerk my hand back so fast you would've thought I'd been burned, and I scramble to my feet. Dog startles and scuttles to the back of his kennel. A blue-shirted employee — not a volunteer — female but with broad shoulders, a ponytail, and thick eyebrows, is frowning at me. I recognize her from months of coming here.

"That's a law-suit waiting to happen, kid. Those dogs are quarantined. Can't you read?"

Blushing, I slip beneath the rope again, staring at my feet. "Sorry. I was just...that dog..."

"Isn't available yet."

"I know, but—what's his story?"

She inclines her head to look over my shoulder. "Someone found him on the side of the road and brought him in."

"With his leg already messed up?"

"Yep. The vet thinks he broke it and it never got looked at, so it healed wrong and...well, looks like that." She folds her arms. I think her name must be Bertha or Dottie or something. She looks like a Dottie. "He's still under a doctor's care for that ear of his. If you're interested, give the front desk your information and we'll call you."

"No, that's not it." I walk alongside her as she leads

me out of the kennels, casting glances over my shoulder even after I can't see the dog anymore. "I was just dropping off some paperwork..."

"For an adoption?"

"A job."

She stops. I stop. She squints. It dawns on me that being caught in an off-limits area was probably not the best first impression to make if I want to work here. Grimacing, I offer out the application I've been carting around. The edge is a little crinkled from how tight I've been holding it. The lady takes it, skims over the first page, and then gives me a weird look.

"You ever had work before?"

I shake my head no.

"Then why should I give you a job?"

It takes everything I have not to respond with *You shouldn't. Sorry for wasting your time.* I bite sharply at the inside of my cheek. The pain blossoming there makes me focus a bit, drags me away from the edge of an anxiety-attack.

"Because I've been coming here for two years to spend time with the dogs anyway, so you might as well put me to use."

A smile tugs at her mouth. Very briefly. She waves the papers. "We'll be in touch."

She leaves me standing outside the kennels and I'm not sure if I nailed that, or completely and utterly failed it. For that reason, I'm not so sure I'm going to mention this to anyone just yet. I don't want Adam getting his hopes up, then being disappointed when he finds out I didn't get the job.

His bike is chained up outside when I get back to the apartment. I still get the weirdest little feeling in my stomach when I see it there, knowing Adam comes home every single night to be with me. We always eat dinner together, even if we aren't very good cooks and usually order out to spare ourselves the embarrassment of making crappy meals. We watch movies on the laptop, or play games on my tiny television.

And, sometimes, he leans over and brushes his mouth against my cheek, or my ear, and I'm beginning to be not so terrified to do the same thing to him.

I have a *boyfriend*. Even if we've never verbally given a name to it.

I'm smiling as I push open the door and step inside.

Adam being in the kitchen is a weird enough sight that it takes me a second to figure out what he's doing.

"Are you cooking?"

His head snaps up. His pale face is flushed, a bit of sweat dotting his brow. "You weren't supposed to be home yet."

"But I am." I start into the kitchen once my shoes are off, but Adam points his spatula — we owned a spatula? — to ward me off.

"Not until it's done."

I take a seat on the edge of the bed to watch him instead. "What compelled you to cook?"

"Don't know." He looks from what I think is a printed recipe to the stovetop and back again. He burns his hand twice and drops food on the floor. But it's kind of amazing, seeing him put so much effort into something the way he does when he plays guitar.

Casper would love this. Adam, trying something new. Adam, comfortable enough — with *me* — to not let fear of failing keep him from doing something.

I really want to kiss him.

He serves me stir fry on paper plates with apple cider in plastic wine glasses that make me laugh. We eat dinner across from each other on the floor and pretend it's a romantic date at some overpriced restaurant, complete with neatly folded napkins. The food is surprisingly good.

We lie in bed with the TV on and we kiss more than I

think we've ever kissed before. The only thing better than staring at Adam's mouth is kissing his mouth, because it's warm and soft and shy like he is, and it's exciting to think no one else has ever gotten to do this before.

Adam likes to slide his hands under my shirt and trace my spine. I like to run my hands through his hair. It is a slow process, this physical aspect of *us*, like we are afraid touching will somehow shatter something vital we need to breathe.

But it's okay like this. Moving slow. One step at a time. We fall asleep early because I'm spent from working up the nerve to turn in my application and Adam is tired from his experiment in the kitchen, and we are both exhausted because we're doing our best to be strong, to be better.

When I wake up, it's to the sound of Adam near my feet and the button-mashing of a controller. He's playing a game. I roll onto my side to face the television and brush my fingers against Adam's leg. He smiles, even if he doesn't for a second lose his concentration. Only when the level is done does he twist around to look at me.

"Morning."

"I don't know how your accuracy is so high on that tiny screen."

Adam shrugs. "I miss my flat-screen from home sometimes."

He lies across my legs. I grunt at the weight, wiggling my toes against his side. "Was it, like, *your* TV?"

"Yeah. I guess. I bought it with Christmas money last year."

"If it's yours, you should go get it."

Adam looks down at me, frowning behind his mop of dark hair. "Should we...?"

"I don't know." I squint. "Wouldn't your mom have a problem with that?"

"She's never home. I still have a key. It *is* technically mine. So is the computer, for that matter."

I push myself up to my elbows, amused. This is something Corey and I would have done. Like when we broke into her ex-boyfriend's car one summer and took his stereo because he refused to give back her CDs. (It startles me to realize I am thinking about her and it doesn't feel like my heart is being carved from my chest.)

But Adam, who couldn't even look his mother in the eye and tell her to go to hell until only recently? I marvel at the small differences between this Adam and the Adam I met months ago. Maybe it's bad that I'm almost giddy at the idea of going back to his place, but—"I did really want to smear jam on the carpets."

All is silent at Adam's house. The maid only comes on Thursdays. With Mrs. Rockswell's car absent from the driveway, we're golden. Adam lets out a sigh of relief when he unlocks the door. Guess he was worried his mom had changed the locks.

We take the stairs to his room. He tries the door and—

"It's locked." He steps back. Stares. Tries again. Jiggles the handle. "She fucking locked the door to *my room*."

"So you wouldn't come back for your stuff, I'd bet," I say. Adam looks at me, lost, before a defiant and frustrated scowl crosses his face. He turns back to the door, plants a foot into the carpet, braces his shoulder against the wood, and slams into it with enough force to rattle the artwork hanging on the walls.

I can't help but laugh.

Adam tries again, wincing. I move up beside him,

pressing my side to the door. "On the count of three..."

Our weight combined cracks the door jamb and it swings open so fast we end up in a tangle of limbs on the bedroom floor. When we pick ourselves up, I head straight for the TV to start unplugging cables. He goes for his computer desk and laptop to do the same.

"This isn't stealing, right?" Adam mutters. "I mean...I'm breaking into *her* house."

"It's not breaking and entering if you have a key," I say, slinging the power cord over my shoulder. "I think."

"You think?"

Shrug.

I meander around the room, fetching any little thing I think Adam might want. An Elvis pen from his desk drawer. A rolled-up Beatles poster from a top shelf in his closet. The jacket he complained about not having awhile ago when the one he usually wears didn't match his outfit and Casper told him he was worse than a girl about his clothes.

When we're done, I have a backpack full of stuff, the poster tucked under one arm and Adam's laptop in my hands, and he's carefully carting his television downstairs. I give a longing look toward the kitchen, but decide it's probably not worth dealing with Mrs. Rockswell reporting my jam vandalism to the cops.

Take away a woman's son and she gets pissy. But ruin her carpets and all hell breaks loose.

The rest of our day is spent playing video games on the new TV and marveling at how much difference high-definition makes. Adam is usually better than I am, but I don't mind much because he always seems so genuinely surprised and happy he's good at anything.

After dinner, Adam surprises me by asking if I want to go jogging. He *never* goes with me. When I say yes, he hands me my coat and says, "Let's go to the bridge."

It's not even six o'clock and the sun is already vanishing, nothing more than an orange sliver against the skyline. We park and jog down the rarely-used bike trails to the bridge, across it, stopping at its center. I can pinpoint the exact spot where Casper crawled over and was prepared to jump. The precise area we all huddled together.

For a moment, I am lost again. Holding onto the railing like I might fall over the edge if I don't. Adam curls his fingers around the rail and stares out over the water and the sunset. "Can I ask you something?"

It's been a good couple of days. I'm not sure I want to talk about anything heavy. But this is us *trying*, right? So I say, "Okay."

"Are we all right?" he asks

This could very well be a trick question. I turn, back leaning into the railing. So cold. "In what way?"

"As in...is this going to be okay? Are *we* going to be okay?"

I don't have the courage to look at his face because his eyes are too honest. "I don't know. I think so. Is that good enough for now?"

Adam shoves his hands in his pockets, toeing at the ground. "I meant what I told my mom. I want to get into therapy." Pause. "I want you to, too."

"I've been to a doctor before," I protest.

"Not all doctors are the same. That was then. This is now."

I'm aware, but are they different enough? Speaking to the doctor Maggie took me to, there were talks of hospitalization, of BPD or manic depression, of a lifetime of medication. If that is what lies in store for me, I don't want to hear about it.

Will I ever know, though, if I don't try? And am I willing to try for Adam?

We stand toe-to-toe on the bridge, neither of us

looking at one another. Aware he is worried about me, and also aware he's in no state to be worrying about anyone when he's trying so hard to get himself stable.

Finally I say, "Harold gave me a number to a therapist. She said she would see us, free." That is what pro-bono means, isn't it? I forgot to look it up to make sure there weren't any hidden catches.

Adam chews on his bottom lip. I hate when he does that. He has a pretty mouth and shouldn't ruin it. "We could try."

I sink to the ground, elbows on my knees. "I don't know if I can do it."

"That's why it's called *trying* and not *doing*. I'll be here to help."

"I shouldn't need help."

"Everyone needs someone sometimes, Vince." Adam crouches in front of me. Somehow his hands are plenty warm when they come to rest over mine. "Everyone. You and I can do this if we stick together. We don't deserve to be this fucking sad. None of what you've gone through is your fault."

I lift my head to meet his eyes.

Not my fault.

Isn't it?

No one has ever told me that before.

It's not your fault your parents gave you up. It's not your fault the foster homes wouldn't help you.

It's not your fault Maggie and Casper died; there was nothing you could do.

My hands flip over, palms-up, fingers wrapping around Adam's warm hands. He doesn't have to stay, but he does. Not because he has to, but because he's worried. Because he *cares*.

I've never been a person who gets over things easily. I've never forgiven the foster homes who kicked me out instead of asking *what's wrong? What can we do to make this better?* I don't forgive Penny for making me feel horrible at Maggie's funeral. I don't forgive Casper for not telling us we'd never see her again. Or Adam, for kissing me and making me wonder why anyone like him would ever look twice at someone like me.

But maybe I need to try.

SUICIDE WATCH

December

SUICIDE WATCH

CHAPTER 31

Me: The shelter called me.

Adam: !!!???

Me: I got the job.

I do not know how to talk to people. It's a good thing my job at the shelter involves dealing more with the animals than the people there to adopt them. I spend six hours a day, a few days a week cleaning kennels and litter-boxes, filling food and water bowls.

My favorite part is getting to take the dogs for walks. By the third day, they recognize my face, and they know when I show up with a leash in hand, they're getting out for a bit of freedom and fresh air. Every one of them is happy to see me.

Now that I work here, I've been allowed some contact with the dogs in quarantine. Every day I've gone in to see the crippled dog. Yesterday, I got to be the one who brought him into the vet's office for one last check-up on his ear before he was given the all-clear to be moved out on the floor with those ready for adoption. Today is the first day I'll get to take him for a walk.

When I stop outside his kennel, hanging with his paperwork is a slip of red paper that reads *Adoption Pending*.

I give it nothing more than a passing glance even as every inch of me begins to ache with loss. It's a good thing, isn't it? He's been out here less than twenty-four hours and he already has someone who's fallen in love with him, who wants to take him home and make him part of their family.

SUICIDE WATCH

Maybe someone who will put forth the money to get his leg operated on and fixed.

(I refuse to let it sink in. Not just yet.)

Dog bounces around, pausing only long enough for me to hook on his leash, then he darts out the gate, circling around my legs and nearly tripping us both. I reel him in, guiding him to walk beside me like I've seen the other employees do, and lead him for the exit.

Outside the shelter is a public dog park, but in the back are the runs only we use. I shut the fence behind us, unhook him, and watch. Dog sniffs at the grass around his feet, stops, and looks back at me, questioning.

"It's grass, genius." I fold my arms. "Go on. You're supposed to run."

Dog's tongue lolls out of his mouth.

"Run. Be free. Roll around. Whatever it is dogs do." I grab a Frisbee from a plastic tub of dog toys, wave it in Dog's face, and fling it. The Frisbee goes a measly six feet and hits the ground. The very first time I've ever thrown a Frisbee, and it's an epic fail. Awesome.

But Dog hobbles over and sniffs at it, so I pick it up and try again.

This time I must've done something right, because the Frisbee tears across the dog run. Dog's ears prick straight up, and he takes off after it.

He doesn't run well. In fact, he mostly pulls his crippled leg up and runs with only his other three. But it's still something watching him tear across the grass. He hops up, manages to snag the Frisbee in his mouth, and crashes down with a resounding *thud*. I jog over to make sure he's okay. By the time I reach him, he's already rolling back to his feet and chomping happily on the disc. I take a seat and scratch behind his ears, rub his stomach, let him occasionally abandon the Frisbee in favor of licking my hands and arms.

I want to cry because he's going away, and I am so torn because he'll be happy and that's important, but I had so much else going on that I didn't prepare myself for him to leave so soon. Even if I knew it was inevitable.

When I take him back to his kennel for the day, I wrap my arms around his neck in a tight hug. "You'll make your new family really happy."

I want to think that, somehow, I was able to help him while he was here. Maybe I helped him be a little less afraid.

I want to think he'll remember me.

"His ear looks better," Adam says behind me.

I twist around while getting to my feet. "Hey. What are you doing here?"

Adam shoves his hair out of his face. There's a plastic bag hanging from his arm from the record store, so it's safe to say he came straight from work. "It was slow. They sent me home. You're off soon, right?"

"Twenty minutes." I hesitate, a smile pulling at my face. I want to kiss him hello, but I'm not sure that I should. He's better at this whole being-affectionate-in-public thing. I get too paranoid about drawing attention to myself. Yet one more thing on my list of stuff to talk to Dr. Dumar about.

Seeing as he has no problems with it, though, Adam leans in and presses his mouth against mine. Briefly, lightly, just enough to satisfy himself. A compromise.

"Let me finish up a few things and I'll be right out," I say, ducking my head because I know how red my face must be.

Adam lets me slip away and I head into the back. I've finished all my work, so it's a matter of killing a few minutes washing the dog-smell off my hands, clocking out, and getting changed back into a regular t-shirt instead of the work-issued blue one.

As I'm grabbing my coat, Helen—the broad-shouldered lady I gave my application to who wasn't actually named Bertha or Dottie at all—pops her head into the back room. "Thought I'd let you know that dog of yours is getting ready to head out with his new family."

I freeze, one arm in my coat sleeve. "What?"

She inclines her chin in the general direction of the lobby. "If you want to say goodbye, you'd better hurry up."

I dart past her, fumbling to get my jacket on, heart hammering in my chest. I'm not ready for this. I've been trying really, really hard—five days without crying and counting—and I don't want to ruin that. I don't want to break down and disappoint Adam or Helen. My shoes squeak on the linoleum as I round the corner, past the kennels, breathing so hard I'm sure my lungs will burst.

At the front desk I spot Dog, wagging his tail a mile a minute. He catches sight of me and begins pulling at his leash like a fish on the end of a line.

The leash Adam is holding.

I stop a few feet away. Breathing hard. Staring. Unsure what I'm seeing.

Adam stops what he's doing and turns to look at me. In one hand is a pen. In the other is the red slip of paper. *Adoption Pending.*

Oh.

Dog jerks at his leash again and this time Adam lets him go. He crashes into my legs, trying to jump up on me but without the balance to do so. He's a good thirty-five squirming pounds, but I scoop him up and let him go to town sniffing and licking my face and hair.

Adam says, "I only have enough for half the adoption fee. So, you know. We'll split him and he can be both of ours."

I don't know what to say. I'm not sure I can say anything without crying.

Instead I set Dog on the ground, step up to Adam, and take the pen so I can sign the paperwork.

"Vince."

I lift my gaze to meet his.

"A dog is a long-term thing," Adam says, studying my face like he might find some trace of what I'm thinking there. "If you aren't totally, completely, *really* sure, don't do it."

A long-term thing. Not just one or two years, but a decade. More. What happens after that?

Life, says a quiet voice in my mind that sounds a lot like Casper. *Life* happens after that. The thing Casper and Maggie were robbed of way too early.

What Adam is offering me, asking me, isn't just *let's have a relationship and a dog*, it's so much more than that.

Have a life with me.
Fight with me.
Fix things with me.
Everything will be okay because we'll make it okay.

It won't be easy. It will hurt and it will ache and there will be days yet to come where I'll be so sad I can't think of anything except *being sad* but—maybe, now, I will be able to look at Adam and look at our dog and the life we're struggling to build, and realize something comes after the sadness.

I sign the adoption papers.

Then I grab Adam's face in my hands and kiss him.

Adam smiles bigger than I've ever seen him smile.

We take the dog outside, Adam's hand gripping mine tightly. On the steps leading up to the shelter he says, "What should we name him?"

We study our weird-looking dog, with his crazy eyes, lolling tongue, crooked ears, and missing leg. Anyone who saw him would think—

I say, "Let's call him Fubar."

SUICIDE WATCH

From: Vincent H. <herecomesthesun@beemail.com>

To: C Harms <enigmaticism@kooncast.com>

Subject: RE: Darling Boys

Casper,

I think I like my job. I like the animals. It's still a miracle I managed to get it, but wouldn't you know it, Helen—the lady who hired me—has seen me there several times before? Guess I'm not as invisible as I think I am.

Adam and I are seeing Dr. Dumar twice a month. She's very nice. She says we might feel worse some days because it's forcing us to address things we don't want to. I like that she isn't determined to medicate me.

Every other week, we also go to Harold's for dinner. Sometimes his new girlfriend joins us. She works at a chiropractic office near his work; he met her after going in because he pulled something in his neck taking out the battery in the van for me. How's that? I inadvertently got a couple together. He's happy. I like that.

Fubar is settling in. My lease is up soon so we're moving into a larger apartment. (It has a real bedroom!) It'll be right next to the park so we can take him for more walks.

Peter Felix (Harbinger's real name, did you know?) was arrested and convicted of nine counts of voluntary manslaughter, and one count of first degree murder. I don't know how it all works. He didn't go to sentencing. They found him dead in his cell. Kind of figures, doesn't it? But he won't be around to hurt anyone and I think that's more important than anything.

We go to the bridge every week and miss you.

Once upon a time, I lost everything and I was so alone. The sadness, the hurt, it all seemed so infinite. When you're wandering alone in a storm, you can't see the end, or if there even is one, and how close it might be.

I'm still wandering, but maybe I don't feel so lost now.

I'll keep trying. I promise.

-Vinny

SUICIDE WATCH

Acknowledgments

Of everything I've yet to write, this book was the hardest.

I get very attached to my characters, and to really express what they're feeling (even when they, themselves, don't know how to express it) is draining and heartbreaking. This book isn't meant to preach or to school, but simply to follow the journey of those who could be saved...and those who could not.

As always, a thank you to my beta readers: Nyrae Dawn, Christa Desir, and Jolene Perry. I'm so humbled to have such talented writers and friends who take the time to read my work to both praise it and help me make it the best it can be.

Thank you to everyone who helped in all the other ways, be it with reviews, cover reveals, last-minute edits, or simply telling a friend to help spread the word. For indie authors, there truly is nothing that helps us more than the kindness of people like you.

It's been angsty, fun, and — I hope — will leave you thinking for a bit.

Cheers,
Kelley York

SUICIDE WATCH

About the Author

Once upon a time, Kelley York was born in central California. And it's there she still resides with her lovely wife, step-daughter, and an abundance of cats, while fantasizing about moving to England or Ireland. She has a fascination with bells and animals, is a lover of video games, Doctor Who, manga and anime, and likes to pretend she's a decent photographer. Her life goal is to find a real unicorn. Or at least write about them.

Kelley is a sucker for dark fiction. She loves writing twisted characters, tragic happenings, and bittersweet endings that leave you wondering and crying. Character development takes center stage in her books because the bounds of a person's character and the workings of their mind are limitless.

You can find Kelley on the web at www.kelley-york.com.

Printed in Great Britain
by Amazon